SIMEON'S
PROPHECY

SIMEON'S PROPHECY

A NOVEL

ANNE TREVETHICK

Simeon's Prophecy
Published by Anne Trevethick
New Zealand

© 2019 Anne Trevethick

ISBN 978-0-473-49999-0 (Softcover)
ISBN 978-0-473-50000-9 (ePUB)
ISBN 978-0-473-50001-6 (Kindle)

Editing:
Rachel Ross & Andrea Candy

Production & Typesetting:
Lizelle Windon & Andrew Killick
Castle Publishing Services
www.castlepublishing.co.nz

Cover Design:
Paul Smith

Dedicated to Lois Woollett,
a special woman in my life.

CONTENTS

PREFACE

Twenty-nine years ago, after I gave my life to the Lord, I undertook a Bible study with my pastor. This involved, as you can imagine, many amazing discoveries and a close involvement with the stories I found there.

The story of the Nativity, in particular, drew me in, and I agonised as it progressed to Christ's death.

While I was still studying, a retelling of the life of Jesus started going through my head, as if someone was dictating it to me. I ignored it for a time, but then started listening; the narrative was usually more prominent in the night.

I began to write it down. When I reached the fifty-seventh page, I came to the crucifixion. I couldn't continue – it was too painful – so I put the story aside.

Many years later, after I achieved my BA in Biblical Studies, I wrote my testimony but, once I had completed that project, I felt bereft; my writing was finished. What should I do next?

I remembered the story of Jesus that had, by now, been sitting for twenty years in my 'to-do' basket. The crucifixion episode was still difficult to write, but once again the words were given to me in the still of the night. The narrative was told from a different perspective – through a mother's eyes – and I felt certain that our Lord wanted people to read it.

That story now appears in this book. I hope you find it as fulfilling to read as it has been for me to write. May it draw you closer to the love and life of Jesus.

Anne Trevethick

CHAPTER 1

DEVASTATION

I left Martha's house early that morning – I couldn't sleep. I had spent the night restlessly tossing and turning, alternately crying and questioning God. Sleep would not come, so I got up, dressed, and went outside. I walked quickly away from Martha's home and started out for the place where I knew Jesus and His disciples often stayed when in Galilee.

The cold night air swirled about me, causing me to shiver violently. The darkness surrounding me only seemed to enhance my pain and confusion. My thoughts were occupied with the events of yesterday; events that drove me out here in the early morning light, unable to sleep or endure the thoughts that filled my mind. All I could think about was my beloved son Jesus. Yesterday I had watched Him hanging on a criminal's cross and I had seen Him die. My mind kept conjuring up His beloved face as He hung on the cross, and I pictured again and again the evidence of the violence that had been used against Him.

My body craved warmth, but my mind was focused on Him. My only thoughts were of my son. I cried into the empty darkness, 'Why, why? What use is He dead? He can't heal or teach when He is dead.'

It was in darkness, just like this, that my son went up the mountain to pray. 'To speak with my Father' is what He always told me. I thought He was crazy going out so early; His days were so busy, with people crowding around Him, calling to Him, begging to be healed. How He loved them. 'They are like sheep without a shepherd,' was His explanation to me. I loved Him so much and worried about Him all the time. In answer to my concern, all He would say was: 'I must be about my Father's work.'

Here in this cold darkness, here where He spent time with His disciples, I thought I could be close to Him again. With the dawn not yet breaking, and the early morning mist still caressing the tops of the trees, I felt His presence.

The birds hadn't stirred yet, and the cold dawn air touched my feverish face with gentle, welcoming fingers. Emptiness filled my soul. I was desolate; my beloved son had been taken from me.

I shuddered at the suddenness and the cruelty of His betrayal. One of His own disciples had betrayed Him to the Pharisees. Alone, my anger burned. 'Why?' I screamed into the emptiness again and again.

The sorrow and loss were unbearable; my body ached, matching the pain in my heart. I sought shelter under a tree. I must have slept a little though because, sometime later, I sat up exhausted and leaned back against the tree. Its rough bark pressed painfully into my back, my thoughts still raced unchecked. How I longed for the echo of His footsteps, the touch of His hand and the sound of His voice. The agony of my loss overwhelmed me.

Lost in my thoughts, I failed to see the sunrise or even to hear the birds which were usually quite vocal when the sun came up. After a while, I became aware of the sun's warmth and, looking up, realised it was another day – but it wasn't like every other day; no longer would I be listening for the sound of His footsteps, nor rejoicing at the sound of His voice. This time the day would not welcome my son, nor would I welcome the day.

CHAPTER 2

MEMORIES

I sat listening to the sounds of the villagers starting their daily round of chores when suddenly, to my surprise, a shaft of sunlight shone through the branches of the tree, striking me full in the face and blinding me for a brief moment. Startled, I looked up, still deep in thought, and heard a gentle voice calling my name just as it did all those many years ago.

'Mary, Mary; you knew all this was going to happen. Remember Simeon's prophecy?'

I cast my thoughts back to the day when old man Simeon, a righteous and devout man well known in the Temple was walking in its courtyard. Seeing Joseph and me, he came across to us and, taking my baby in his arms, said, 'This child is destined to cause the falling and rising of many in Israel and to be a sign to be spoken against, so that the thoughts of many hearts will be revealed – and a sword will pierce your own soul too.'

How right Simeon had been. I now understood what he meant. My heart felt as though it was pierced, broken, and bleeding. The voice was now silent, or was it just my mind playing tricks? Whatever it was, it got me thinking about the past.

Were memories the way I could bring Him close again? I remembered what Jesus had said – that He would rise on the third day – but how foolish that seemed to me now. Shutting the door on the memory of my son's death, I slipped ever so gently into another time, a time when my son was alive and still with me. I wrapped my shawl tightly around me and let my mind drift back, back to when I was just an innocent young girl, betrothed to a man called Joseph.

CHAPTER 3

AN ANGELIC
ANNOUNCEMENT

I was blessed. Father had chosen for me a wonderful husband; his name was Joseph, and he owned a carpentry shop in the village. Joseph was older than me. He was well-respected, a kind, gentle person, and I was smitten the first time I laid eyes on him. Everything about him made my heart beat a little faster. I think Joseph felt the same way too because he teased me gently about my unbound hair. A bride price had been negotiated, everything was settled, and our betrothal ceremony took place. I excitedly looked forward to our marriage. However, it didn't quite go the way I had planned.

I thought about the morning that changed everything. I felt again the low windowsill against my legs; I had been sitting looking out over the village dreaming of my upcoming marriage, and I saw again the young man who appeared in my room. All around him blazed a strange light, and I heard once again the words that would change my life.

The light from the young man was shining so brilliantly that I had to look down at the floor. He told me that I was favoured of God and that I was to bear God's Son. All kinds of emotions filled my heart – fear, joy, unbelief – and I thought of the strangeness of this encounter.

Here was I, a young girl kneeling before a strange man in shining garments, and I was asking a very pertinent question: 'How will this be, seeing as I am a virgin?' The angel, as I now knew this young man to be, said to me: 'The Holy Spirit will come upon you and the power of the Most High God will overshadow you.' My heart still thrilled at those words.

After the angel left, I went to see Joseph. I told him about the angel, but my courage faltered a little bit when I told him about the Most High God overshadowing me, and that I would be with child and have a son. I was fully aware of the consequences of such a statement. Our laws were very strict in a situation like this. I was betrothed to Joseph, and this would be like confessing adultery and making up a story to cover my sin. But how could I ignore God's commandment? I was very sure that it was God who commanded me.

Joseph was shocked, as I knew he would be. Quietly putting down the mallet on his workbench, he turned to look at me. There was astonishment on his kindly face as he asked me, 'Could you please repeat what you just said?' I did so, my voice trembling.

'I thought that was what you said.' He spoke quietly, gravely, yet to me it was like thunder, and the ground lurched beneath me. Ever attentive, he put his arm around my waist, and I leaned gratefully against the warm solidity of him.

'Mary, what can I say? I must pray about this.' He looked up and said, 'The sun is high, and it's very hot. Go home. I will come and see you in the morning and tell you what we will do.'

'We' – my heart beat hopefully; Joseph had thoughtfully coupled us together, but that night I couldn't sleep. My thoughts kept going round and round. If Joseph dismissed me (which he had every right to do), I would not only be disgraced, but I would die. Death by stoning was the only answer from our law for the betrayal of one's betrothal promise.

CHAPTER 4

WHAT WAS TO BE
MY FATE?

That afternoon was one of the worst in my life. Mother wanted to know if Joseph and I had been fighting. I told her I was just tired and not to worry, and that I would be going up to lie down and would see her at supper. The afternoon dragged. I could not face any of the things that I was preparing for our wedding, so I just sat at the window and stared out over the village.

Supper duly arrived, and I went downstairs. Although I was not very lively and talkative, Mother and Father hardly noticed. Talk of the upcoming wedding flowed around me, and I answered with as much enthusiasm as I could. Although I was tired I could not sleep that night. It was hot and airless, so I opened the window wide and continued my anguished pacing, relishing the cool night air on my fevered face – yearning for the sun and yet fearing what it would bring.

As the darkness faded, I stopped my pacing and sat in the window. The stars were still bright and shining. The darkened shapes of the palm trees shivered slightly in the cool night breeze. Were they in sympathy? Did they know? My mind was made up, and I whispered, 'Thy will be done, Oh, Lord, Thy will be done.'

Heavy in heart, I stayed quietly on the windowsill look-ing out into the fast-approaching dawn. I was still sitting on the sill when the sun came up, but I didn't think as I usually did – willing each day to come and go, making my wedding day come closer. Today my heart was burdened and each hour only deepened my desolation. The warmth of the sun heated my skin, but not my heart. It was gripped by a deathly chill.

Around mid-morning, I heard my Mother talking down-stairs. She had not called me this morning as she usually did. My footsteps in the night as I paced my room must have wakened her. She probably thought I must be sleep-ing. I listened through the window, and my heart missed a beat. It was Joseph! I heard Mother's steps on the stairs, and then there was a gentle knock on my door. 'Mary, child, Joseph is here to see you.' I thanked her and told her I would be right down. I rinsed my face in the bowl and wrapped my shawl around my shoulders, hoping my reddened eyes were not going to betray me. Then after a silent prayer, I went down the stairs to where my Joseph was waiting.

He took my arm and guided me out to the seat beneath the date palms. I quietly sat down. His face had looked so grave that I felt the need for something solid underneath me. I fixed my eyes on the warm sand beneath my feet. A small dung beetle walked slowly by. I sadly chased it with my toe. As it moved forward, my toe would follow close behind it. My whole world was concentrated on the morn-ing walk of a small brown beetle.

Suddenly two brown feet came into my vision, and a finger lifted my chin upwards. 'Mary, Mary, you are not lis-tening to me.' I looked into his serious face and noted his very brown eyes, flecked with those interesting specks of gold that I so loved. His eyebrows were thick and already peppered with a few greying hairs. His lips were beautifully shaped, and his skin was so brown. I loved him so much.

A little tear formed in the corner of my eye and again Joseph repeated, 'Mary, you are just not listening to me.' I looked down at the sand, shook my head, and tried desperately to concentrate. The little brown beetle had disappeared. I had nothing left to focus on, so I looked up and saw that Joseph was smiling at me.

'Mary, something strange happened last night. I was praying about our situation and trying to come to a decision on the best thing to do. I tried to think of the best way to break our betrothal quietly, so no one would know the reason.'

I looked up at him. His concern for me, even after he thought I had betrayed him, made the tears that had been threatening spill over once more. Joseph looked at me again and placed an arm around my shaking shoulders. 'Mary, that was what I was thinking; I just didn't want any harm to come to you.'

'Well, as I was saying, an angel appeared to me and said, "Joseph, son of David, do not be afraid to take Mary home as your wife, because what is conceived in her is from the Holy Spirit. She will give birth to a Son, and you are to give Him the name of Jesus. It is destined that He will save His people from their sins."

'Mary, I was so sure that it was a dream, but I now know after the angel spoke to me that the baby you are carrying is truly from God. So, Mary, we will still be married, and you shall still be my wife.'

I stared at Joseph in amazement. Had I heard correctly?

I was still to be his wife – not sent away in disgrace. I was to live? I looked up, searching his face. He was smiling at me, and I knew then for certain that God had provided for me. We were safe. Jesus and I were to be cared for.

As the realisation of this seeped into my conscious-ness, I was suddenly aware of the birds singing and the sun warming my skin. I couldn't speak, but the love I felt for Joseph overwhelmed me, and the tear which threatened to fall from my cheek was gently wiped away by a strong warm hand.

I took hold of his hand and just stood there, waiting for the realisation to sink in. My marriage was still to happen. I was not going to be sent away or, worse than that, be stoned to death for betraying my betrothal contract. Joseph still wanted me as his wife.

The excitement that had left me after the angel's visit suddenly came back to me, and I spun around under his arm and said to Joseph, 'I must go, I have so much to do to prepare for our wedding.' Joseph smiled at me and let go of my hand. Shaking his head and with laughter bubbling from him, he turned and walked back to the village.

When I got home, Mother saw my face and laughed, 'So everything turned out alright – no more arguing?'

Giving her a quick hug, I said, 'No, no more arguing Mother,' and rushed up to my room, eager to get back to my embroidery and to finish the last item needed for my wedding chest.

CHAPTER 5

OUR WEDDING

At long last it was my wedding day. The days seemed to go by so slowly that I thought it would never come. I peeked out of the window, willing it to be a sunny day, for we expected quite a few people. Well, actually, almost the whole village was expected, and our wedding feast was to be held outside under the trees. I breathed a huge sigh – yes, the sun was shining. I stood shyly as Mother came in and gave me the usual 'prior to your wedding' talk; I smiled at the serious look on her face. Nothing could turn me away from this glorious day. I listened with as much care as I could as she listed the problems or joys I could expect as a wife.

I skipped outside to look over the preparations being made. I praised the Lord for the sun, for Joseph, for my serious mother, for my wonderful father. I thanked Him for everything I could think of, my arms raised in joy.

I knew Joseph had finished our home, and the waiting to see him and my new home was painful. I loved him so much and couldn't wait to be his wife. I heard the music and singing in the distance, as I sat being ministered to by my mother, who just now tugged on my unruly locks, begging me to sit still. How could I sit still when all my dreams were coming down the road right now to claim me? However, like a good daughter, I tried.

Finally, I was ready. Flowers were in my hair, my carefully embroidered dress had been dropped over my head, and my dowry headdress of coins and jewels was pressing uncomfortably around my forehead. My veil was in place, and my stomach was quivering. 'Nerves,' my mother said when I told her. 'You will be fine when Joseph arrives' – and she was right. When he entered the house, all I could do was sigh with pleasure. He looked so handsome in his wedding finery.

Our wedding day was perfect. The house Joseph had prepared for me was wonderful, and I proudly placed all the things I had made around my new home. 'My home' – I ran the words over my tongue again; it sounded wonderful.

As the days wore on, and my life settled down as Joseph's wife, I desperately wanted to tell my cousin Elizabeth about the wonder that even now was beginning to make itself felt.

The calls of the children down in the village brought me out of my reveries and back to the present. I stretched, easing out a stone from under my knees and then I leaned back onto the trunk of the tree. I gratefully sank back to the time where pain had no substance and the future seemed so bright.

CHAPTER 6

ELIZABETH'S MIRACLE

I had to visit Elizabeth. I had to tell someone what had happened to me before I burst with joy. Elizabeth was the only one I could tell; this news was not for my mother, not just yet. The angel Gabriel had told me that Elizabeth was also with child. She would understand everything I told her because it had happened to her also. Elizabeth was known to be barren and yet... oh, this was so exciting! Elizabeth was my cousin and, to a young girl like me, she was old and would need help for a while. The daily work would be very hard on her as she got closer to the birth. Anyhow, that was the reason I gave to Joseph. He was not happy that I wanted to travel at this time, but I wanted to be with Elizabeth, wanted to sit and talk of babies, births and heavenly beings.

Joseph had arranged everything perfectly. Our donkey had a soft new saddle to ensure a comfortable trip. He had purchased a new water bag and gifts for Elizabeth. One of his friends was to accompany me on the trip, to care for the donkey and to protect me on the road. I didn't like the fuss. I just wanted to be alone, to soak up the joy and wonder of it all. Joseph's wise arrangements, however, made me realise that my trip was not completely without danger. Joseph was afraid for me but, although the trip was arduous, I was young, healthy and enthusiastic. At last we were off. The sun was high, and it was going to be hot. Our donkey daintily picked her way along the steep and stony paths, and the swaying motion caused me to drowse.

I thought about everything that had happened to me, but particularly of the Father's provision for the baby and me. It was peaceful here on this part of the journey. We hadn't yet reached the spot where we would meet the caravan trade with its camels and people, so I welcomed the chance to dream of the future.

I went over in my mind all the things that had happened to me, from the first meeting with the angel Gabriel to hearing about Elizabeth and her expected child. I was thrilled to hear how someone as old as Elizabeth, who was way past childbearing years, had been favoured and chosen by the Lord, just as I had been. I was also keen to hear how the angel had spoken to her – what he said and, if I was honest, what he looked like. Was it the same angel who spoke with me?

My mind raced ahead, and I was anxious to see my beloved cousin again. We had always been very close. I had shared her despair at her barrenness, and now I could share her joy, her wonder, and her excitement. Oh, I did so long for this journey to end. My body was beginning to ache. Donkey saddles were not the most comfortable things in the world; we had been in the hills for three days, and even my youthful exuberance was deserting me!

'How much farther?' I kept asking my husband's friend.

'Not too much longer,' he answered. 'We should be there by evening.'

I nodded off again, dreaming of angels and little babies. We arrived at the time he said we would, just as the light faded into evening.

Elizabeth's house, with the light shining from it was so welcoming, and her arms so warm, but her greeting amazed me. She said that I was blessed among all women and blessed was the fruit of my womb! A joy such as I had never known encompassed me and praise to the Lord flowed from my lips. My heart felt as if it would burst! I couldn't express the joy that I felt, but Elizabeth knew the feeling, for she had also been blessed.

I stayed with Elizabeth for some time, helping her with those never-ending chores. We talked and praised the Lord – it was a lovely time for us both. We endlessly discussed our encounters with Gabriel, with Elizabeth tirelessly telling me of how Zachariah had not believed and had been struck dumb by the angel. Afterwards, the angel had said, 'Your prayer has been heard, and your wife Elizabeth will bear you a son. You will call him John.' 'John' – she voiced the name again and again, delighting in that name.

I can still see her face. It was glowing like a new bride, as she contemplated a son after all these years and, most wonderful of all, the Angel of the Lord had named the baby John. The name didn't feature among our generation, but John was from the Lord and was a special little baby. He would be a delight and a joy, and many would rejoice at his birth.

The time passed all too quickly and, regretfully, I headed for home. I would have liked to be with Elizabeth for the birth of her son, but her time had not yet come, and I yearned to see Nazareth and Joseph once again. I sent word to Joseph, and he sent his friend back to bring me home. Once again, I climbed on the back of our gentle donkey, and we wound our way through the mountains to Nazareth.

I finally arrived home, tired but happy. Not long afterwards, word came to us that Elizabeth's John had been born. A discussion had begun among the relatives about the name Elizabeth had called her son. Later she told me what had happened and what the relatives had said. She told me that her eldest brother had said, 'We have no Johns in our line. I don't know where you got that name from; it's not right, you can't name him John.'

The debate flowed on into the night, until suddenly there was a rustle of paper and they all turned around to find Zechariah, Elizabeth's husband, writing frantically. As they looked over his shoulder, they saw that he had written, 'His name is John.' Zechariah's face was alight with joy. He had a son, just as the angel had promised. Most precious of all, he had a voice again. His throat was a little rusty from lack of use, but the joy that came bursting from his mouth was full and musical. How wonderful are the ways of God; He accomplishes all that He intends, our destiny is in His hands. All we have to do is obey.

CHAPTER 7

CAESAR'S CENSUS

S ome time later, Caesar Augustus, the Roman Emperor, sent out a decree that a census should be taken throughout the nation. All the people had to gather at their ancestral homes to register. My thoughts were of the taxation that this census might bring upon us. I knew that taxes were necessary for the upkeep of our roads, but I also now knew that our carpentry trade did not bring in very much. We worked among very poor people who could not pay very highly for the work Joseph did. Still, a decree was a decree, and you ignored the call at your peril.

My time to give birth was very near; I was terrified that I would give birth on the road, but my gentle Joseph reminded me of the fact that my life and the life of my son were in God's hands. He was sure that little Jesus would be born safely and not in some dangerous mountain valley with brigands around every bend, or wild animals in every unseen cave. Very gently, he admonished me, 'Trust, my dear one; trust in God's care and rest in His arms.'

Once again, our donkeys were laden with food and water, and we turned their heads towards Bethlehem. Both Joseph and I were of Davidic lineage so, even though I was married to Joseph, I was still obliged to register in Bethlehem under my own name. The trip this time was very unpleasant, and the road teemed with people going to Bethlehem.

Children were everywhere. The dust was thick and, as the weather was hot and dry, shade was not very plentiful. Our water had to be shared out very carefully; it seemed to evaporate through the very skin of the bag itself. I was worried that each well we stopped at would be the last with clear water in it. The number of people with whom we shared water grew daily.

The villagers took donkeys, cattle and even goats with them. These animals would help with food and milk on the long journey. The flies and the stench were sickening to me. I pulled my veil tight around my shoulders and my face, hoping to shield my face from the flies, dust, and the sun, only to shrug it off as the heat became too much for me. It made me sway dizzily on my precarious perch.

CHAPTER 8

NO ROOM AT
THE INN

My size stopped me from being at all comfortable and, though I worried for our poor little donkey, she seemed to realise my plight and trod very delicately. Even though the saddle was bumping me continually, the pain I was now feeling was not her fault.

I prayed that we would get there in time, for something told me that Jesus would not wait much longer. After a day or so, I took to walking a bit – Joseph led the donkey, with his arm about my swollen waist, almost carrying me as we continued toward our destination. After we reached our next night stop, I told Joseph that my giving birth was not too far away and that I didn't think we would reach Bethlehem after all.

'Mary, I have been worried about you for some time. You are so pale – why didn't you say something? We could have stopped and rested.' I shook my head, gripped by another pain which threatened to tear me in two. Reaching for his hand, I gratefully slid to the ground, but another pain came as I looked up into his worried face.

'Joseph, can we find an inn or something – anything that is away from all these people?' I cried out as another pain told me this was now an urgent matter.

Joseph understood the situation quickly. 'I can see a village up ahead; can you hold on till then?' I heard his voice from far away but felt his arms lift me back onto our patient donkey's back.

'Hurry Joseph! We must go quickly; my time has come.' The little donkey must have felt my urgency and my pain, for she trod quickly but carefully towards the village Joseph had seen. The donkey's lurching gait magnified my pains, and I involuntarily cried out. Joseph turned to look at me and helplessly lifted his hands towards me. 'No,' I whispered, 'Keep going, we must reach the safety of the inn. I cannot give birth here. Please keep going.'

Joseph put his head down to our little donkey's grey drooping ear. 'Come little one,' I heard him say, 'We have a mission today. Jesus must not be born on the side of the road – let us hurry, but be careful; there is precious cargo on your back.'

The last few miles were a blur, as I tried hard to keep the pain from overwhelming me. I clung to the saddle horn with all my might; I tasted salt on my lips and realised I had bitten them through with the effort of keeping silent.

Suddenly we were at the gateway of the inn, and the well-lit courtyard was a welcome sight. The donkey was now standing still, and I lurched forward into the waiting arms of Joseph. We knocked on the innkeeper's door. I was near to total exhaustion now, and the pains were coming regularly. Joseph was holding me up, and then the door opened, and the innkeeper's concerned face came into sight.

'Oh, dear lady, I am sorry we cannot help you here, we are full.' I looked up at Joseph; the tears that had threatened were now coursing down my cheeks unchecked.

'There is a shelter over the rise against the hill. It has animals in it, but it will be quiet, and the warmth of the animals will keep the shelter warm. I am so sorry, but it is all I can do. Everyone is here to register, and all my rooms are full.'

I didn't want to hear any more.

'Joseph, quickly let's go, hurry or it will be too late, and I will give birth on the doorstep of this inn.' I longed for my mother, for her warm encompassing arms and for her quiet steadying voice. I shut off the thoughts and started to walk away, grateful that I had Joseph. We had to hurry – birthing was a natural thing which wasn't restricted by time, and my time was now on me. I heard Joseph asking the innkeeper to hurry and get in touch with the village midwife.

We finally came to the shelter, and I looked around for a place to put baby Jesus on His arrival. I was in despair as the only place I could find was the manger filled with straw, and the animals were still eating out of it. The manger was filled with fresh new straw so, as long as the animals moved away, I felt it would be okay. I turned and saw a pile of straw in the corner; I quickly made a bed out of it, then turned towards Joseph whose strong, warm arms surrounded me and, lifting me off my feet, he laid me down on the sweet-smelling hay.

Many years later, the smell of fresh, warm hay brings me back to that traumatic time. The innkeeper, keeping his word, had called the village midwife who, although astonished at the surroundings in which I lay, kept her peace, placed her equipment on the ground and began preparing for the imminent arrival of my baby. Through the waves of pain, I could see Joseph's face full of concern and pain too.

I gripped his hand, and everything receded, apart from those very brown eyes that speckled so interestingly with gold.

My whole universe was those eyes; I focused on them, relished them, and drowned in them. Suddenly the pains ceased, and I became aware of the cry of a child. The King of the Jews, God's Son, and the Redeemer of all Israel had arrived and, after the midwife laid Him in my arms, I just stared in wonder at Him. He was so beautiful, so perfect. He stared back at me solemnly, as much as to say, 'Well here I am, now what?'

The midwife wrapped Jesus in the swaddling clothes we had brought with us and gave Him to Joseph, saying, 'Where will He lay while His mother sleeps?' That was the last thing I remember, and I fell into a deep sleep, exhausted by all that had happened.

Some time later I awoke. Realising that my ordeal was over, I sat up, leaning on an elbow, and looked around at my surroundings. I was in a rude shelter, in the company of some animals that were quietly standing by the manger. I could see our donkey, an ox, a little colt, some goats, a cow and Joseph. All of them were staring into the manger. On one side was a wooden stall where donkeys could be tethered out of the wind. On the other side was a bucket for water, and of course the pile of straw from which I had made my bed.

I lay back on the straw, contented that at last the pains had gone. I was no longer swaying atop of our little donkey's back. I sat up quickly; where was my baby, was He all right? At that moment, I caught the eye of Joseph, who quickly came over to my side. 'Ah, the little mother is awake. Mary, look! See the animals – they just stand there looking into their manger, and they won't leave His side. He isn't scared. He just smiles up at them as they slowly chew the cud, not moving, not dipping their heads into the manger, just standing around Him watching. They must be hungry, the night is so cold, but that is all they are doing, just watching.'

It was then that I noticed how cold it really was and started shivering. Joseph immediately pulled my cloak over me, adding his own cloak to keep out the chill.

'Joseph, is Jesus warm?'

He smiled at me and said that the animals were keeping away the chill. 'It is amazing. I wonder if they know who it is in their manger. Do they understand that their Creator is the baby lying there?'

I looked at the animals. Each one was staring into the manger – our donkey, the colt, the ox and the cow all circled the little manger – yet Jesus did not make a sound. No fearful whimpers as all these strange creatures stared down into His face, and I marvelled at the gentleness of the creatures gathered there.

CHAPTER 9

VISITORS IN THE
NIGHT

I must have slept for a while, leaning gratefully against the warm shoulder Joseph had offered me when suddenly I woke with a start. What had I heard? I was conscious of bandits, and I knew wild animals were in these parts. I shook Joseph awake.

'Listen,' I whispered, 'I hear voices coming up the path.' I was concerned we did not have much in the way of protection; indeed, we did not have much of anything, and at that moment, we were very vulnerable.

Joseph looked down at me. 'Mary, why are you afraid? There is no one who can harm us. Remember, we are under His protection.'

I smiled up at him gratefully and as I did so, saw a small boy's head appear at the opening of the stable, and then a man's head, followed by two others. They carried staffs in their hands and slingshots at their waists and as I saw their woollen cloaks, I realised that they were shepherds.

One of their number came forward, and Joseph went to meet him. They talked together for awhile, and I saw Joseph nod his head and turn towards the manger. As if by an unseen command, the animals which had ringed the manger parted, and the shepherds crowded around staring into the manger's depths.

Joseph came back to me and told me a wonderful tale about how Heaven had announced Jesus' birth to the shepherds of Bethlehem. I was stunned at his words. God had announced His Son's birth to shepherds, announced to the humble and poor people of Israel that their Saviour, their King, had been born. His Son would be known as the Shepherd of Israel, so to shepherds the birth announcement was made. It was fitting that a shepherd should be the first to welcome Him.

All of this was buried deep in my heart, the amazing wonder of it all. I thought about the angel who had visited me, the dream that ensured Joseph would still marry me, the long trek we made from our little village home to our arrival here in this stable. The King of the Jews was born in a stable and visited, not by other kings, but by shepherds. I smiled at the ways of God.

I watched the manger, surrounded by animals and people, and marvelled that so many could squeeze into such a small space. Then the noise of all the people struck me. Listening, I heard nothing from the baby; then Joseph came over and in wonder said, 'Jesus isn't frightened by all this noise. He just looks up at them and smiles. Shouldn't He be crying? Isn't that what babies do? I thought that too much noise frightened them, you know, made them unsettled.'

I looked at the concerned face of my beloved husband and said, 'Joseph, remember He is God's Son, and these are His people, so He doesn't fear them.' I moved over a little to let Joseph join me on the straw, and together we watched the amazing sight of animals and shepherds all kneeling together to worship our son.

The days slid quickly by. The newness of being a mother never left me, and I fussed around my infant, looking, touching, and rearranging His coverings. I never tired of holding Him in my arms. Just watching that little mouth smile brought me such joy. My Joseph was so proud. He also could not get enough of that sweet little face, and I knew if he went missing for a while from his workbench, I would find him cooing over the little cradle he had made for Jesus. He was so protective of both of us. It was so funny seeing the crease that appeared across his worried forehead whenever Jesus whimpered which, I might add, wasn't too often.

CHAPTER 10

THE LAW IS
FOLLOWED

On the eighth day after our son's birth, Jesus was circumcised as the law required, and finally officially named. All too soon, forty days had passed, and it was time for my purification rites, also required by our laws, so once again we set out for Jerusalem and the Temple.

We set off early in the morning as, not only were my rites to be completed but also our child was to be presented to the Lord. Our little donkey, now more serene, picked her way carefully up the path to Jerusalem.

The morning was still very cool; we had started out early so that we could beat the heat of the sun over the mountain passes, but the sun blazed uncomfortably over the dry, dusty passes just a little while after we left. We then entered the road which led out of the village and into the mountains. The wind blew the dust into everything, and the glare from the sun made our eyes feel as if they were full of grit. The scant vegetation gave no shade, and the flanks of the mountains sent the blown dust down to the valley like a waterfall.

In some places, the size of the hills on either side of the passes kept the sun at bay for a few hours and the morning dew still sat in the shadows under the overhanging rocks, giving the pass an icy feel.

I gratefully pulled my cloak about Jesus and clutched Him tightly as we lurched down yet another steep incline. The donkey's delicate hooves caught on the sharp little rocks half hidden in the soil, making a gentle clicking sound that, if you were not aware, could lull you into a dangerous stupor.

Jesus slept peacefully in my arms, lulled by the donkey's swaying gait; I sat with Him in my arms thinking about Jerusalem. I loved the busy city – what girl didn't? – and the beautiful Temple never ceased to amaze me. I was a country girl, and there was nothing in that great city which didn't amaze me. We didn't venture away from home this far unless we had an errand that couldn't be dealt with in our little village.

In the city of Jerusalem there were many people; tradesmen plying their wares, soldiers with their shiny armour, beggars in their pitiful clothing and high-ranking citizens with their attendants all rushing hither and thither, and the noise! Animals, people, stallholders crying out their wares, women at the water fountains – the noise was incredible; everything in your own thoughts became a jumble. Bethlehem was a small town in comparison to Jerusalem; although, to a small-town girl, even Bethlehem was an enormous thriving city.

My body trembled with excitement, and the little donkey faltered. Joseph let go of her reins and came around to see if I was seated properly. 'I thought I saw the girth strap slip a little,' he said to me.

'No, Joseph, all is well,' I answered. 'I think I will walk for a while though.' With that, I handed Jesus down to Joseph and slid down the side of the donkey until I was on the ground. My knees buckled a bit, as I had been seated on the donkey's back for so long, but I was over the ordeal of Jesus' birth and strong again.

CHAPTER 11

JERUSALEM

As we approached the top of the next rise, Jerusalem was spread out before us. The rolling hills and gardens and the clumps of olive groves on the outskirts of the city with its clay houses looked like a tapestry of greens, yellows and browns. From the height we were at, the sun's rays seemed to be like fingers pointing out the beauty below just for us. Here an olive grove, there a few houses, and over there, the sun glistened on some water.

I caught my breath as the Temple shone out like a beacon. The walls of the Temple were white and gold, causing the building to glimmer in the still air. We stopped and stared, spellbound.

Joseph picked up the reins of our donkey who, taking advantage of the rest we had given her, was nibbling on the foliage at the side of the road. He said to me, 'Mary, it's midday, you must be weary. See that clump of trees over there, just a little further down the rise? We will stop there, and you can tend to Jesus in the shade. I think He is a bit hungry; He is sucking his thumb quite hard.'

I looked at Joseph gratefully – the promise of a rest was just what we needed. We had been on the road since dawn, and the sun was now very hot. I could see that Jesus was getting restless. I was getting hungry as well. We could eat in the shade, and I could feed our son, who obviously needed changing.

The clump of trees grew by a small stream, this being the reason they were still green and not stunted like the other clumps of trees we had passed. I relished the muted shade after the bright sunlight, and the cool stream would supplement the warm water we had in our wineskins.

Joseph unloaded our packs from the back of our donkey, allowing her to go down to the stream to drink and graze on the plants that were there. I sat under the branch of a large olive tree and gently unwound our son's swaddling bands. I bathed His face with some of the water from our wineskin and put Him to my breast.

As He suckled, I stared in wonder at this child. His eyelashes traced small circles on His cheeks. His nose was tiny; His head covered in soft, downy hair. I touched my own dark locks and wondered what colour His hair would finally be. His tiny hand was curled around my finger; His fingernails were like small pearls. I had not seen a pearl, but I was sure they would look like my son's fingernails.

This beautiful child was God's Son! Could I care for Him correctly? Could I guide Him through His childhood until it was time for His Father's work to be done? I shivered at the tremendous responsibility Joseph and I had been given and prayed for the Father to help us in this great task. I looked over at Joseph, who was unpacking our lunch; he would be a wonderful father figure for Jesus. He was caring, strong and loving, and between us we would take on this task of loving God's Son. We would shield Him until His time came. Jesus would learn Joseph's trade; a carpenter was always needed, and it was honest, hard work. He would live among the poor, would be taught the Torah and be a good son. He would have loving, caring parents until the time came for His visit to the Temple at twelve years of age. We would not fail at this great task.

I looked across at Joseph, who had just called my name.

'Come, Mary,' he pointed at the lunch things and the blanket he had laid out under one of the trees. 'Mary, come and eat. I have drawn fresh water for you, and the goat cheese is ready. I found some figs on the fig tree over there and I picked them for you. I know how much you love figs.'

I smiled at his thoughtfulness, rewound Jesus' swaddling bands and whispered in His tiny ear, 'Joseph will make a wonderful father for you and you will be taught how to make beautiful, strong carts and ploughs. He is a craftsman,' I said proudly, 'And he will protect you until you are ready to fulfil your mission.'

I was rewarded with a sleepy smile as Jesus fell asleep. Joseph was right. The figs were large and juicy, the birds had not yet tasted their delightful flesh, and the fresh water was cool, clean and sweet on my lips.

'I wonder why warm water tastes so terrible?' I asked Joseph, but Joseph didn't answer. He had eaten and was lying full-length under the trees, eyes closed and breathing heavily. I smiled and decided to let him rest as he had walked for a long time, and we were within sight of Jerusalem, which lay just beneath us. I looked over at the donkeys; both our donkey and the pack donkey were safely hobbled and were grazing quietly under the trees. I sat with my back up against the rough bark and watched while my family slept in the midday sun.

It was pleasant under the trees. The shade was cool after the heat and dust of the road, and I could hear the gentle tinkling of the water and the crickets with their constant buzzing sound. The crickets must be in the shade of this tree. I couldn't blame them.

The mountain road at midday was neither good for man nor beast; all who travelled on it sought shade and rest at midday.

Joseph stirred slightly, and I noticed a large fly hovering near his face. I picked up a frond of grass and flicked it away. 'Sleep, my beloved, I will watch over us,' I whispered.

I let him lie there for a while longer, then reached over and woke him up, playfully kissing the tip of his nose. 'Did I fall asleep?' he asked. 'You should have woken me up because there are zealots around these parts.'

'Hush,' I said. 'All is well; they also must rest when the sun is high.' We packed up our baskets, rescued the donkeys by the stream and were on our way again in a very short time.

The road continued down towards Jerusalem. We passed fields and groves of trees; these were gentler on the eye than the stark bones of the unforgiving road winding down from the mountain passes. We were entering the fertile valley, and I could see olive groves, trees and gardens, and – excitingly – the entire city, dominated by the Temple sitting high above it.

As we travelled closer to the city, we could see the people flowing in and out of the gates. It was then that I heard the noise of humanity, which would soon drown out our conversations with its constant all-encompassing din. Jerusalem was the heart of Jewish pride and a source of deep religious significance; people from all over Judea came to do business and attend the Temple. Our laws and religious rites insisted on our pilgrimage after the birth of a child. But to me this was a joy, not an insisted-upon religious task.

How excited I was! Spilling into Jerusalem were booths and stalls with all sorts of tempting goods but, as we were poor, I knew the money securely held in Joseph's purse was for the dedication of our son, not for feminine fripperies. Nevertheless, I could look and admire, and this I did – feasting my eyes on all the wonderful sights. It was exciting soaking up the buzz of voices and languages as Joseph led the donkeys through the golden gate into the city.

Once in the city, we wound our way through streets which were often blocked by beggars. My heart wept for them, with their sores and missing limbs and their pitiful cry of 'Alms! Alms!' They never ceased to tug at my heart strings, but we had as much money as we needed for my purification rites – and not a shekel more.

From my seat on the donkey's back I marvelled at all the buildings, but shuddered as the shadow of the massive Fortress of Antonia passed over my body; it left me with a sense of foreboding that I didn't understand, and I was grateful when we had passed it by. The sun flooded over me when the fortress disappeared from view, and I noticed we were not far from the Temple itself.

CHAPTER 12

SIMEON'S PROPHECY

The Temple stood at the top of the hill, its walls towering above the city. As we approached, the crowds grew more intense. So much activity was going on that my neck was suffering from constantly being turned from side to side, trying to see everything. I was overwhelmed by the priests and their attendants as they hurried up and down the sweeping marble steps to the Court of the Gentiles. I couldn't wait to enter those steps myself, but first we must take the cleansing ritual bath called a mikvah before we would be allowed up those sweeping marble steps.

After completing the mikvah, we ascended the steps to the Court of the Gentiles, intent on the purchase of two pigeons. Doves were out of our price range, but first we had to change our small coins into Tyrian shekels, the only currency allowed for Temple offerings. The money changers were usually seated under the pillars supporting the walls that surrounded the Temple. We headed across the courtyard to change our money, the people and the ensuing noise flowing around us like a vast sea. I was almost overcome by the heat and leaned gratefully on Joseph's arm; we were almost across the wide courtyard when an old man stopped in front of us and held out his arms for my son.

I looked at him carefully. His eyes were kind and his face gentle and, as he took Jesus from my arms, he looked up to Heaven and his words went deep into my heart.

'Sovereign Lord, as you have promised, you may now dismiss your servant in peace, for my eyes have seen your salvation which you have prepared in the sight of all people, a light for revelation to the Gentiles and for glory to your people Israel.'

The old man then turned to both Joseph and me, staring in wonder, and blessed us; but his next words chilled my heart. 'This child is destined to cause the falling and rising of many in Israel and to be a sign that will be spoken against, so that the thoughts of many hearts will be revealed, and a sword will pierce your own heart too.'

What did he mean? I sensed a loss, a loss so great that I didn't think I could bear it. I took back my son and clutched Him tightly to me. 'I will protect you, little one, have no fear.' I didn't know, I just didn't know how that prophecy would affect me. We thanked the old man and continued on towards the money changers, when suddenly an old woman whom I recognised as a prophetess came towards us. She also gave thanks to God and spoke about our son to all who were there, all those people who had been looking forward to the redemption of Israel.

These two old people filled my heart with wonder and, if I was honest, with a little fear. They were recognising my son as the One sent to redeem Israel. I praised God for His goodness and, burying my fear deep in my heart, turned and went up the steps with the two pigeons Joseph had purchased for my purification.

CHAPTER 13

BETHLEHEM

J oseph and I returned from the temple in Jerusalem to our little home in Bethlehem when everything required of me by the law was fulfilled. I was grateful to be home again, although happy to have been to that great city. I had found it noisy and I thought it overpopulated with so many people, but now I was content in our own little home.

In the days that followed, our child brought us so much joy. He grew strong and healthy and our lives began to settle down after the harrowing trip before His birth. And after the revealing prophecy in the Temple courts of Jesus' calling, peace was all I needed.

The little town of Bethlehem provided this peace. Bethlehem was small. The people there were farmers who needed Joseph's carpentry skills. Jesus could grow up and learn his earthly father's skill. He would go to the Torah school like all the other boys until He had grown and the time for Him to begin His Heavenly Father's work arrived...

It was only a short time later that we heard of the strange visitors. The well was a good place to hear all the latest news and it was said that the strange people, obviously kings, were visiting Herod looking for a king. I made all the right noises with the rest of the women over this news, all the while marvelling at the play of the sunlight over my son's limbs as He lay in the shade of the palm trees.

It was hot and I had laid Him under the trees in the shade but, as the breeze shifted the fronds of the palm tree, the sun hit His flesh and His legs would kick in glee, His little hands trying to grasp the sunbeam which shone on His upturned toes. His smiles could light a darkened room, and my heart ached with love for this beautiful, dark-eyed baby. He was my baby, and I marvelled that such beauty could come from me.

The prophecy and the chill were buried deep in my heart. I thought no one could hurt us until God called for His Son to begin His work, and that was a long time away. I picked up my water jar and went over to gather up my son and head for home. I had flour to make, goats to feed and a meal to prepare; there was no time for talking.

It was hot and the wind was warm, but not very pleasant. It seemed to lift the sand just ahead of me and swirl the gritty pieces into my sandals, making it uncomfortable to walk. I was very glad to see the outskirts of our humble village and then finally to go through the door to our little home. Jesus had slept peacefully all the way home, and I gently laid Him on His small bed. I smiled at the chubby little legs which stretched out as they touched the cool surface.

I turned and attended to my chores, humming gently.

Life was certainly pleasant. Our home was small but adequate, and Joseph had a good trade going. A carpenter was always needed in a farming community. Then there was my son Jesus; how I loved Him. He was a good child, and His smiles and attempts to talk delighted us both immensely.

CHAPTER 14

KINGS, CAMELS AND
WORSHIP

Later, in the early dusk, I heard a strange noise; it sounded like a camel train, and that was strange as camels were not usually around this area of Bethlehem. The noises reminded me of the women's talk at the well. Strange kings had gone to Herod looking for the King of the Jews. The village was seething with the story. Did the kings know about my son, and had they heard of the prophecy at the Temple made by Simeon?

When anything real or imagined threatened my son, the chill that I felt settled in my soul. I turned from the small compound and went into the house, turning up the lamps fully to disperse the shadows which were making grotesque images on the white plaster walls of our home.

With the noise that our few animals made, it was always difficult to hear the sounds outside, but I distinctly heard the tinkling of bells and a low chanting. There were camels outside; I discovered that as I looked out the window.

More importantly however, they were in our compound. I stared in wonder at the richness of the tableau I could see. I had never ever seen clothing so beautiful and so vivid in colour. The saddle cloths, reins and tethers were lavishly ornate, shimmering with precious stones and fine embroidery.

A few simply-dressed men were milling about; they were obviously not the owners of those camels. Maybe they were the attendants – yet, even though their dress was simple, I could see that the style and cut of their clothes were not of this country.

It was now evening, and I stared in wonder as the moonlight caught the jewels on one of the camel's reins. I gasped as a myriad of colours flashed like fire. Joseph had arrived at the window; he also had never seen anything like this before.

Suddenly Joseph pointed, and I saw that there were more men behind the simply-dressed camel drivers, who were now heading for our pathway. There were three of them, and such was their poise and confidence that, even before I saw the camel attendants bow before them, I knew they were men of considerable importance.

I had never seen anyone like these men before. The richness of their clothing had me staring in wonder and fear.

Joseph told me to open the door as the men were now walking up our path. 'Mary, you are staring. These men are our visitors and we have certain etiquettes to attend to.' His voice sounded sharp. 'Go, get them some water and bread. They have travelled far by the look of them.'

I rushed to do my husband's bidding, making sure Jesus was safe in His bed before gathering dates, bread and my newly-made goat cheese, quickly laying them out on our small table. I then went for our water pitcher as the first visitor entered through our doorway.

He was so tall that he had to stoop to enter, the lamplight reflecting off the jewellery that hung around his neck. I gasped. His skin was as black as the night and his face was without facial hair. I looked at him in wonder, until a sharp cough from Joseph shook me from my trance and I hurried on my way for the water, feeling embarrassed.

When I returned, Joseph was talking to a man with a long beard, so I stood off from the group for a while, just watching these strange men with their gorgeous clothes and unusual features. Where did they come from? Were they from the lands beyond Egypt? I knew of the riches of Sheba and Persia from our Torah. Then I remembered what the girl at the well had said, 'They are looking for the King of the Jews,' and my heart stood still. They were looking for our son, I just knew it. What did they want with our son?

I turned quickly and gathered up my child, noticing how the tall black man watched my every move.

'Mary, bring our child,' said Joseph. 'These men are from the East, and they have been following the star which their writings said would lead them to the King of the Jews. Mary, the star led them to our door. Come, bring the child. They have travelled far to see our son.'

I shyly moved forward into the pool of light shed by our lamps and stood in the middle of the room, our son in my arms.

The three men stepped back as they saw Jesus and then fell on their knees and worshipped Him. After a short while, they beckoned to their attendants, who then came forward carrying boxes. When they were opened, the light from the lamps shone into the boxes – one contained gold, another contained frankincense and the last contained myrrh.

I trembled, immediately recognising the symbolism of the myrrh. Death – myrrh meant death, and my mind flew back to Simeon's prophecy. Once again, my heart was filled with dread and my body shivered with the realisation that this was the second time that Jesus' destiny was prophesied. Mercifully, these things were far away, and my spirits lifted as the three kings gave the gifts to my son in recognition of his kingship. I thought of the angel Gabriel's prophecy which said, 'He will be great and will be called Son of the Most High God.'

That period of time was an end and a beginning for me – an end to the bliss of my quiet home with Joseph and my baby, and the beginning of a journey which would end in my son's death and a broken heart for me.

CHAPTER 15

THE FLIGHT TO EGYPT

Early in the morning, Joseph shook me awake. The sun had not yet risen and the moon's light still shone through our window. He said, 'Mary, we must leave this place now.'

I replied, 'Now?' and asked Joseph, 'Why right now? It's still dark!'

Joseph pulled me to my feet. 'Yes, right now. As I slept, the Lord appeared to me in a dream and told me Herod is seeking our son. He is going to kill Him. We must obey immediately.'

'But where will we go, Joseph?'

'Mary, the Lord is sending us to Egypt,' answered Joseph.

Egypt! A shudder went through me. The journey to that land was not only arduous, it was also a long distance away. The tales of our ancestors always filled me with dread. Egypt had always been a refuge to our people in times of distress.

'How did Herod know about us?' I called over my shoulder, as I packed our meagre belongings.

Joseph, busy with the bedding and with the packing of our donkeys, said, 'Remember the three kings told us that they had visited Herod and told him of their writings concerning the new king? They didn't know his true feelings as they talked with him. Fear not, Mary – the Lord has once again provided a way out for us. Now please hurry. Time is important, and we must be gone before the day begins.'

I quickly gathered our things. As I picked up my sleeping son, I saw that Joseph had already prepared our donkey with my saddle, and the pack donkey was nervously pawing at the ground. Joseph went to the donkey and calmed her with a soft voice and a gentle hand. Before the sun had risen, we quietly left Bethlehem.

We heard later how the kings had been warned in a dream of Herod's real intentions and had returned to their countries by a different way. Herod was furious. His next actions were unthinkable. He sent his soldiers to kill all the babies under two years old in the village of Bethlehem and its vicinity. If we hadn't left earlier in the night, Jesus would have been killed, and I would be desolate and weeping uncontrollably, along with all the other mothers in Bethlehem. I praised the Lord for the life of my son, whilst weeping for all those mothers who had lost their sons because of Herod's fury.

The next years were long and lonely. Sure, I made friends with the women at the well who gathered water and washed their clothes by the river, but they were not my family, and not my mother. I yearned for her gentle voice, her arms of comfort and her ready smile.

However, I said nothing to Joseph. I worked at my allotted tasks and watched my son grow. I watched and waited for the call to return to my place of birth, to the rolling hills and the little villages where my heart was resting.

A few years later, we heard that Herod was dead, and

an angel appeared to Joseph, telling him we could now go home. I was beside myself with joy at the news. I longed for the sound of my native language, longed for the synagogue of my own little village. Bethlehem, however, was not in our Lord's mind. Although Herod was dead, his son Archelaus was now reigning in Judea in place of his father – and Archelaus was more dangerous than his father had ever been.

CHAPTER 16

HOMEWARD BOUND

Joseph, who had been warned in another dream, turned our donkeys' heads towards Nazareth instead of our beloved Bethlehem. I didn't care – Egypt was behind us, Galilee was calling, my cup was once again full.

Nazareth was so different from Egypt, although Egypt was fertile thanks to the river Nile. It was a land of plenty, but its cultures and idol worship unsettled me. Its people were easy to get to know and Joseph's carpentry talents were always in demand, but Egypt was not our home.

We settled quite quickly into a routine in Galilee. Joseph went back to carpentry, and I quickly slipped back into village life. I had a lot to occupy me for, after a time, our small family expanded, and I proudly watched my sons and daughters grow.

Jesus, my firstborn, was always special to me. He grew strong and tall, a solemn child, His gentle eyes would follow me as I went about my tasks. He would always be asking questions: 'Why, mother, why?' were words that seemed to be constantly on His lips. He watched me make bread, sweep the rooms, and then, in an instant would bound out the door and go to watch His father smoothing the rough wood on a yoke he was making. I would watch as

He stroked the wood, smiling up at His father, and watched as Joseph's large brown hands would take the childish ones and show Him how it was done. I had said years ago that Joseph would be a good father and I wasn't wrong. Joseph had the utmost patience with his little son, smiling as he answered those constant 'Why?' questions.

Village life was peaceful; we followed the seasons – spring, summer and winter passed for us in a welter of hard work, prayer and feastings, marriages, births and deaths. The patterns of life in a small village eased the fear in my heart, shaping it and pushing it into a small never-looked-into corner.

That is, until the Passover of Jesus' twelfth year. It all started as usual with what shaped up to be an exodus. Every family packed all their belongings to go up to Jerusalem. The village was in turmoil. For many of the young boys, it was to be their first sight of Jerusalem. For others, it would be the beginning of their journey into manhood.

Soon, some of the boys would be twelve and the time would almost be upon them for their 'bar mitzvah', which celebrates their passage into religious maturity. Jesus was fast approaching that time; a poignant time for a mother as her little son was now becoming a man. Although her time alone with Him was drawing to a close, it was not quite yet.

Soon, however, everyone was packed. The village was ready, and we all filed onto the road that led to Jerusalem. The road was full of donkeys, children and animals, and the usual dust cloud that follows crowds on a dirt road started to rise from the ground. All those feet churned up the dust and the noise was stupendous. All the women chatted, catching up on news, greeting new babies. Then there were the children, screaming as they ran around and under your feet. The animals also made their presence felt. You had to watch where you put your feet. Some people went barefoot, others wore shoes, but if your foot landed in one of the messes that the animals left behind, you had to move off the road. It took some time to clean yourself, and then you had to try to catch up with your relatives. It involved a run along the side of the human crocodile until you recognised your family, and then a gentle push and a shove to get back to your place in the line.

All the families travelled together, so there were blocks of one clan – and then other clans following. All the adults knew that the city and Temple courtyards would be a massive crush of people, which we never looked forward to. However, this was Passover week, and the crush was to be expected, Passover being a very important ceremony. It was a memorial to the wonderful gift of life given to us by our God when He killed the firstborn males of the Egyptians all those many years ago and brought us out of our slavery, setting us all free. God's command was that it should be observed for all time. It was a precious sharing time that we looked forward to; we would meet up with old friends and acquaintances at the Temple – that is, if we could find them in the crush.

As always, the festival was a reverent time for all of us. The newcomers to the festival were filled with awe; the old hands were also filled with reverential awe. Nothing about our festivals was boring. The colour, the trumpets, the priests, and of course the Temple itself were overwhelming.

Pride filled your heart as you realised that you were God's child, and it was your God-given right to be at this festival worshipping your Heavenly Father.

CHAPTER 17

MY FATHER'S HOUSE

When the Passover festival was over, we all turned for home, the whole village travelling together as I said before. We didn't keep our young ones close; they ran on ahead to be with their friends or with their cousins, and Jesus' absence from our little group did not alarm me. The next morning, however, when we searched through our relatives and friends and could not find Him amongst the other boys, we were frantic and raced back to Jerusalem. For three days we hunted for Him, until we found Him in the last place we looked, which was the Temple. The Temple was a very large place, and as we searched through the courtyards, we heard His voice. Following it, we finally traced Him to a room on the edge of the courtyard and there, surrounded by Pharisees, was our son. They were questioning Him and discussing His answers amongst themselves. Frantic as I was, I paused and looked at my son, God's Son.

His brow was unruffled, and He was calm. To be so near to priests and answering questions as He was doing was fearful for every boy starting on the road to manhood – but God's Son took it in His stride.

The calmness in my son was something I had not experienced before – He was, after all, a young boy sitting there among those priests, His dark eyes unruffled, serenely answering all their questions in His sweet childish voice. I could see He was causing the priests a bit of concern. I could hear them whispering, 'Where did this child get such knowledge?' as His answers to their questions flowed from His lips.

The dread that was buried in my heart started to grow; He was still a child, so young, so innocent. Oh, please God – not yet, not yet, a little more time for me to hold onto Him, I love Him so.

I called to Him, 'My son, why have you done this to your father and me? We have been frantically searching for you.' His answer once again nudged the dread in my heart.

'Why were you searching for me? Didn't you know that I had to be in my Father's house?'

I didn't truly understand His answer to me; I didn't want the dread that was beginning to overwhelm me to become obvious to our son, but Jesus obediently got up, said good-bye sweetly to the priests and followed me out of the Temple.

Thus I began to tread the pathway to my greatest dread, the loss of my son to His true Father. Jesus grew in both body and wisdom; He was a delightful child who was turning into a strong, loving individual. As the eldest, He helped in our carpentry business; the heavy work suited Him, His arms and shoulders filled out, and His hands were large and strong, ministering each day to my children and me.

Nothing was too much trouble for Him; He helped all who asked something of Him. He was adored in our village; all the children followed Him about, and He was often seen with a child on His shoulders, or gently soothing a scraped knee. The elderly of our village were never short of a helping hand; they only had to ask and He was there. Poor Joseph would sigh and carry on without Him – so patient and loving was His earthly father.

CHAPTER 18

JESUS' DESTINY CALLS

The years that followed were like a flowing river. All the waters in a river head for the sea and Jesus was like that; He now knew His calling, and all His energy and thoughts were channelled into His coming work.

He heard about John the Baptist and went to the river to hear him preach. From that moment on, my contact with Him was intermittent. Jesus had been baptised by John in the River Jordan, and there were stories about what had happened at the baptism. People said they heard what sounded like thunder and that a dove flew out of the sky and hovered over Him. I heard all this from those who had been there. I didn't see Him after His baptism because He went straight up into the desert. For forty days He was gone; He walked alone. He had taken no provisions with Him and wore only His cloak over His tunic. I was worried for Him. In my heart, I knew He was with His Heavenly Father, or so I thought. However, when He returned, one of the disciples whom He gathered about Him told me of the harrowing time my son had suffered.

As a mother, I was appalled at His appearance when He returned. His face was burnt by the sun, and His tunic was torn in places. I looked at His scraped feet and knees; dried blood had dripped onto His leg, leaving a brown smudge, but it was His eyes that worried me the most – they had a faraway gaze about them as if He had looked on horizons that were not of this world. I knew without a doubt that He was no longer mine. He belonged to His Father in Heaven, and I mourned my sweet little son. His path had been laid down, and I couldn't follow, even if I wanted to.

We both had commitments – for me, it was my family and Jesus; He had his Heavenly Father's will to accomplish. Those dark solemn eyes, no longer childlike, now gazed upon horizons I could not see.

He was now on a mission; touchable, loving, concerned for all who crossed His path, but He no longer belonged to one family. His family now encompassed all of God's children, and for the first time, I felt the pain of loss.

Jesus gently grew away from me; I could feel it in the strange way a mother can when her son's life is shaped by another's will. He was still a loving son, but His times with our family were getting shorter and shorter.

Jesus drew people to Him like a flame draws moths. He gathered strong young men about Him, and they adored Him – Simon, Andrew, Peter, James, John, Matthew and others. He gathered them from all walks of life, from our class of people; simple, unspoiled, passionate men. These men became part of His closest thoughts. I followed in my heart, yearning for the closeness of His childhood, fearing the vastness and tragedy of His future.

CHAPTER 19

CANA – THE FIRST MIRACLE

Then came the day when Jesus performed His first miracle. I must admit, I did ask for something to be done, and I may have forced His hand a bit, but this was a wedding, and the groom was the son of a cousin of mine. They had run out of wine, a disgrace of huge proportions. The social standing of the young couple was in jeopardy.

I knew Jesus was coming, and I also knew He would know what to do. He arrived with His disciples, and I went over to see Him. I told Him of the problem, and His answer was, 'Dear woman, my time has not yet come.' My heart did a little lurch. Had I presumed too much? No, His warm smile persuaded me that I had not presumed, so I ran over to the servants and told them that they must do whatever He said.

In the warm voice that I loved so much, He told them to fill up the water jars used for ceremonial washing. They did this and looked at Him for more instructions. He smiled that tender smile and told them to take it to the wedding organiser, who was at that very moment talking with the groom's father. The servants interrupted the organiser and drew a glass of the water from the stone jars, passing it over to him to taste. A wonderful smile lit up the organiser's face, and he slapped the groom's father on the back, congratulating him on the quality of the wine that was now going to be served. The groom's father had a very quizzical look on his face, at which Jesus and I smiled together. This was His first miracle, and His disciples stared in disbelief. Then, because they knew what Jesus had done, they were like children all talking at once while Jesus looked at them with a fatherly eye, grinning widely.

This was now His time – He was now officially a rabbi (a teacher), and His disciples were His family. I joined them on their many journeys as much as I was able, but I was getting tired and the nights in the open, even though they were around a fire, were not for me. The ground gets harder as you grow older, and old bones feel every little stone.

I was now alone; my beloved Joseph had gone to be with the Lord, but my family had grown and with it my responsibilities as a grandmother. Instead of being with Him personally, I would hear of His accomplishments from others, and I was so proud. Jesus had been gone for a while travelling around Galilee, Capernaum and Jerusalem. Travellers through the village always brought news of the new rabbi and His miracles.

They recounted events from a large gathering at the lake, where my son fed five thousand men and women with two fish and five small loaves taken from a small boy's lunch. They spoke of demons being called out of deranged people, and lepers being healed. How the people loved Him. His movements were followed closely by the Pharisees and Sadducees, but He always managed to outwit them. They were His people's shepherds and yet they were fleecing them and laying huge burdens on their backs with their interpretations of the law. Jesus knew that His Father had not meant for His commandments to be so burdensome. His arguments with them had escalated wildly from the answers He gave them as a child.

The simple people of the villages loved to hear the parables He spoke. They could relate to them. They understood what He told them, and when the stories came back of the parable of the lamp under a bowl or the lost wedding coin, I would smile and remember the little boy following me around as I swept and attended to my cleaning tasks. I marvelled that He remembered them at all.

The tales from travellers was all I had left now. Jesus was journeying far and wide – everyone wanted to be near Him and to see Him, but I, His mother, could only cling to memories. What memories they were. As His popularity grew, His visits home became fewer and fewer.

CHAPTER 20

THE PEOPLE'S
RABBI

Jesus' fame spread like a fire through dry grass, wildly and out of control. The masses who yearned for release from the yoke of Roman control clung onto His every word – words that were never heard of before; He cured their diseases, cast out their demons and brought them hope and peace. This peace flowed out of Him and, looking into His eyes, people's troubles melted away. Yet, just a few moments before, troubles overwhelmed them. Who could resist Him? His earnestness, His love, His concern and His knowledge drew the people. Everyone wanted to learn about this Kingdom of Heaven that He talked about so knowledgeably.

His teachings brought light into their minds; minds that had been in the dark for so long. The authority that He manifested amazed them as He delivered them from demons that had racked them with pain. Who could resist His compelling call to a kingdom of love? Our shepherds – the Pharisees and Sadducees – were harsh taskmasters, piling upon the people laws so strict that they could not drink without the fear of breaking some minuscule law, and therefore offending God. Their God was severe, not the God of love that Jesus showed to them. He brought to them a God that was within their reach, a God who cared about their problems, a God who loved His children and did not constrain and fetter them. Jesus brought them back to the God who had rescued their ancestors, the God who had parted the sea for them and cared for them in the desert for forty years – such was His care that their shoes never wore out in all that time.

The scribes and Pharisees had taken the laws set down before Moses and interpreted them in a way that had chained the people with unnatural restraints, with burdens that kept them in fear, turning them aside from the Heavenly Father who loved them.

How they loved to hear Jesus' stories and parables about His wonderful Kingdom, but the more the people loved Jesus and the more they flocked to Him in droves, the more the Pharisees' anger grew. As leaders of Jerusalem's flock, they feared for their position. If Jerusalem rioted, Herod would send in the army, and their high positions would be taken from them; the peoples' rioting proving they had lost control. They were afraid that Jesus would be made king and afraid that the people, released from the hold that the Pharisees had over them, would rebel and try to replace them with Jesus. Consequently, they began plotting.

I was extremely frightened for my son's life. A woman passing through the village told me about an incident that put Jesus' life in jeopardy. A mob, which included the Pharisees, had surrounded Him. They had dragged a poor girl to Him who had been caught in the act of adultery. This was a death sentence in anyone's language. Looking at the girl and taking in the crowds of people surrounding Him, all of them with murder on their minds and stones already in their hands, my son immediately knew the trap they were trying to spring on Him.

The woman telling us about it all said that Jesus bent His head and looked at the ground. The girl had been dragged half-naked from her tryst, and I knew He would be trying to give her a little dignity, no matter how small. He then started writing in the sand, slowly but with great composure, and quietly said, 'Let him who has no sin cast the first stone at her.'

How clever He was! The trap was met with His usual quiet manner. He didn't look up, the speaker said, but slowly the stones were dropped, and the crowd melted away.

After a little while, He raised His head and asked the woman standing before Him where her accusers were, and she answered, 'Gone, sir.' Jesus then said to the woman that He didn't accuse her either, but she must go and sin no more.

'As they moved away, the anger on the Pharisees' faces was plain to see,' said the woman relating this story to us. 'I heard them all muttering together. I do wish Jesus would be more careful.'

So did I. Fear gripped my heart as, knowing more than she did, I knew that a climax would soon come.

CHAPTER 21

DANGER BECKONS

Jesus and the Pharisees were on a collision course, and I was deeply afraid that things would end in a very bad way for my son.

Oh, why did He anger them so? Of course, He had His destiny, and they had theirs. He was following His Father's will, which was to be Israel's Saviour. He was their Shepherd and not afraid of the marauding wolves.

As a child, He showed no fear, so why should He be afraid now when He was about His Father's work? Nothing could touch Him until His time had come. Until then, He fought for His Father's children. He walked strongly and surely to His Father's call; nothing could sway Him – why? Because Jesus came from Heaven; Jesus knew things of which other people could only dream. Heaven was His home and His guide; the kingdom of men held no fear for Him.

The old man Simeon's prophecy, given at His birth, returned to me constantly and I grew more and more concerned. 'This child is destined to cause the falling and rising of many in Israel and to be a sign that will be spoken against so that the thoughts of many will be revealed.' Well, I thought, He was doing that all right. 'Be careful, my son – oh, please be careful.' I suddenly felt at peace; I knew

He wouldn't be careful, but whatever happened to Him, He would be in the Father's care, just as He was when He was a small child. I didn't know though; I just didn't know. Sometimes God's plans are not as ours would be.

The days flew by, and the word coming from the towns reported that Jesus was going up to Jerusalem for the Passover feast; some thought He was going to be crowned as king. Somehow that didn't feel right but, wanting to be near Him and to be with my son on His journey to His destiny, I gathered up my belongings and headed for Jerusalem.

I had made this journey many times in my life, but not like this time, with many thoughts filling my mind. Some of them were filled with fear – fear for His life. Such was the power the Pharisees had over the people and, close to the seat of their power, the crowds in Jerusalem could be swayed easily. Yet, if reason had anything to do with it, if He were to be crowned as king, He would rid us of the dreadful yoke of Rome and peace could once again seep through our country. Amongst my fearful thoughts were a few gems of pride and joy.

The way up the steep mountain passes was just as I had remembered it, hard and unforgiving. The sun was just as cruel, blinding us at every turn in the steep path. The heat and dust and of course, the never-ending buzz of those infuriating flies made the journey most unpleasant.

I remember thinking the only forgiving factor was that I was not about to give birth. I didn't feel the usual joy though; the anticipation of meeting friends and seeing Jerusalem at its finest, dressed in its festival garb, just wasn't there.

I had trodden this path many times on the way to the festival but never before did my heart beat so fast. Fear was following in my footsteps, and it wasn't very pleasant – fear, not for me, but for my son. Was Jerusalem to be the centrepiece of my son's drama? What on earth was He going there for? Didn't He know there might be trouble for Him? I answered the question in my mind myself – my son and His logical sense of reasoning would have ignored the problem of His safety, ignored the threats from the Pharisees, knowing that His life was in the hands of His Father. Until He had accomplished His mission, none could touch Him.

I had heard all the stories, and my mind went over the latest exciting story told this morning at the last resting-place. I thought about the moment when the breathless man burst into view there on the top of the mountain. He was beside himself as he told us of Jesus' triumphant entry into Jerusalem. We all thrilled at the tale. He told it so vividly that we could almost see the crowd, smell the dust and hear the noise.

CHAPTER 22

THE PHARISEES GATHER

The man's eyes were wild with excitement. He said Jesus had entered the city on a small donkey, and the jubilant crowds had pulled fronds off the nearby date palms, laying them in front of the little donkey. Others took off their cloaks and laid them on the path as the donkey, a little skittish because of all the cheering, stepped daintily over them.

The very thought of people laying precious clothing on the path in front of a donkey seemed over the top, but the messenger was adamant that was exactly what had happened. When the man was questioned about the absurdity of the actions, I blessed the woman who had brought that up – it saved me from bringing the crowd's attention to myself.

I realised that once again I was day-dreaming, in spite of the messenger's exciting story. 'Mary, you are getting old, listen to the man,' I admonished myself and, shaking my head, I tried to concentrate. I listened again and was astonished to hear what the messenger said next: 'The crowd was calling out, 'Praise to David's son, God bless Him who comes in the name of the Lord.' The messenger was excited; his eyes were blazing, and his arms were waving about as he acted out the story for us.

The people gathered around him were swayed by his words. My son's name was on everyone's lips. Some were asking, 'David's son, is He the promised Messiah?' They were all talking at once. 'Is He? Is He our king, our Messiah? Have all the prophecies finally come true? We must hurry, we have to see this for ourselves.' The messenger was pushed aside as they headed down the path towards Jerusalem, with more determination than if they were just going to the festival.

I saw their excitement and thought about this deep need for a king, this zeal for an end to Rome, this expectation, this deep desire, this earnestness – what was it and where did it come from? I paused for a moment, trying to put into words what I had just seen. In my mind's eye, I remembered the crowds in the villages around Galilee and their reaction when He had healed and preached to them. I also remembered how the crowds reacted when they saw something unusual, or when a Pharisee questioned Jesus. The crowds that loved Him just a moment ago could turn ugly in a matter of seconds. As I looked at the comparatively small crowd gathered around the speaker, swaying as one excited mass, I grew cold, and I knew that my son was in danger.

If this small crowd could be made so excited by one man's story, couldn't a similar crowd react in the same way? A larger crowd swayed by the hate encouraged by the Pharisees could become a riot and then... I shook my head quickly, trying to drive away the terrible scenes that were flowing through my mind. I knew that Jesus was surrounded by people at all times; wherever He went, they followed Him. The Pharisees were proud, and they hated the adoration that people were giving Him. The influence that Jesus had over the people worried them immensely.

I had listened to the tales that travellers passing through had brought to the villages; they said that the Pharisees tested Him at every opportunity with questions, which He then answered with parables or with another question, making them look small and insignificant in the crowd's eyes.

The people loved Him, and they loved this Kingdom He was bringing them with His words. A Kingdom in which God ruled supreme; a Kingdom without the harsh Roman rules that now had Israel by the throat.

The crowds in Jerusalem were highly excitable, but they were also pliant. One moment they were applauding you, and the next they were stoning you – I feared the intensity of their emotions. 'How wonderful it would be if you did become king, my son, but they could just as quickly turn against you.'

The Pharisees were against my son. They hated His popularity, and I knew this before I had even seen what they were like. Travellers to the villages always brought news of the big city, and my son's actions were always the first thing they talked about. The Pharisees and Sadducees had tried to harm Him many times, and each time, He had overcome them. His words swayed the crowds, and His actions were applauded.

CHAPTER 23

THE JOURNEY TO
JERUSALEM

It was Passover. The crowds would be flocking to the Temple courts and who would be there to meet them with His words of love, and with His healing? My son! Anything could happen at this time. Many an uprising had been started with less than the antagonism that would be heatedly displayed by the factions that were against my son. My heart was heavy. Something was stirring in my memory, but my mind couldn't grasp it, and I shrugged my shoulders, left the crowd, got back on my donkey and turned her head to Jerusalem once more.

The journey was more arduous than ever this time; the road was a seething mass of raucous voices, pushing people, noisy children and even noisier animals. I just couldn't get through the throng. Each time I tried, I was rudely pushed back with 'Hey! No pushing, keep to your own space!' I had to hold tightly to my basket of provisions to stop them from toppling onto the road – I didn't want them trampled.

I was so glad when I saw the gates of Jerusalem rising above the crowd. Tears were very close now, and I felt dizzy with the noise and heat, but the thought that had eluded me back there on the road had just resurfaced. It was that dreadful prophecy given to me at Jesus' dedication. It had followed me throughout my life, always just below the surface, ready to bubble through whenever I was in fear of His life. The tears that had threatened before now gently trickled down my cheeks, for I had just had a revelation. I knew now what the prophecy meant, and my heart was breaking.

Unaware of where I was, I heard a rough voice saying, 'Hey, watch where you're going woman with that donkey!' I heard the harsh voice from far off; it was a centurion. I had wandered through the gates, automatically leading the donkey down the usual route to my friend's house. We had always stayed there when our family travelled to Jerusalem for the Passover festival. I had inadvertently taken the path which led up to the Fortress of Antonia and had stumbled into the centurion. His cold voice cleared the thoughts from my head, and I looked around. I apologised to the centurion, hastily shifted my basket to the other hip, tugged on the lead rope of the donkey and walked on.

I could feel the walls of the fortress bearing down on me; its stones solidly placed one on the other filled me with dread; its shadows were icy on my skin. I shuddered, quickly pulling my shawl tightly around me. Why did this place affect me so much? I had no idea. I only knew that this place was not welcoming to me. A short time later, I gratefully turned into my friend's courtyard. After I had tied up the donkey, grabbed her some straw from the manger and given her some water, I turned and knocked on the door of my friend's house.

CHAPTER 24

WARMTH AND FELLOWSHIP AT LAST

I fell into Martha's arms as she opened the door. She and her husband had always sheltered our family on each Passover festival. 'Mary! Whatever is the matter? Come quickly, come inside, your face is so white, are you ill? Everything has been prepared for the feast; the upper room has been leased. Jesus has just sent Peter and John to rent a room, and He said to them – now I want to get this right, it is amazing what He said. Oh, I remember – He said to them, "Go into the city to a certain man and tell him the Teacher says: 'My appointed time is near, I am going to celebrate the Passover with My disciples at your house.'" That's just what happened! They found the house, and all of the men are there now preparing for the Passover.'

I felt giddiness come over me again and must have swayed visibly, for Martha steadied me again. 'Poor Mary, such a journey you have had, and I am lacking in hospitality. Please come inside and tell me what is worrying you. Is it Jesus?'

I nodded silently, unable to voice my thoughts.

'Mary, He came in triumph! He rode in as Jerusalem's king. They love Him and want to crown Him. My, you are such a silly girl.' She gently took my hand and led me to the couch. 'Mary, your hand is icy, and you are shivering. Tell me why you are so upset. What is troubling you?'

I only stared at her in mute agony and shook my head as the tears rolled silently down my cheeks.

'Mary, come closer to the fire. Warm yourself. The journey was too much for you. Why did you come so far alone? I know you wanted to be near Him.' I let her carry on with her crooning voice, trying to take away my fear. Yes, I wanted to be with Him for one last time, one last time before... I knew now that this was to be the last time, knew it with all my heart.

The words He had spoken cut through my agony, as I remembered what He had said. 'My appointed time is near.' Those words brought back to me the first time I heard Him talk about His time. But those initial words were, 'My time has not yet come.' Jesus said this time, 'My appointed time is near.'

I knew with all my heart that He was in dire danger, knew that these words meant His death was near; His time had come. It had finally come, and my heart was broken. 'Lord, dear Lord, have mercy, please not yet, a few more years, we need Him so, and I need Him.'

I knew, though, that this time it was going to happen, and the words of the prophecy echoed in my head. 'A sword will pierce your heart.' Yes, I thought, that describes exactly what my heart feels like – like a sword has cut it in two.

There was no reason yet, but still I wept – wept for my son, wept for the loss to the world, for the loss to me, but above all, for the trauma that this would be to His disciples. He loved His disciples more than anything; He was their rabbi and their guide. They were like sheep amid a pack of wolves. I cradled my head in my hands and rocked backwards and forwards, trying to ease my aching heart, trying to stop the thoughts that were tumbling through my mind. I was sure that my heart couldn't take much more, and then a pain ripped through me, and a sudden thought came to me, silly really, but the pain I was feeling now reminded me of the pain I had when Jesus was born. That was in a different place, of course, but this time, it was not going to bring joy, only a loss that mankind would not be able to replace.

The night wore on slowly. Other friends arrived at Martha's house, which was the meeting-place of Jesus' followers and friends. I looked over at the women who followed my son or simply just accompanied their husbands on the journeys Jesus took. I had known them all for a long time now, and they were all good, simple folk. Like most women, their hands were never still. Some had brought their distaff and spindle with them and were busily spinning their wool. Martha was at her loom and every now and again, when the talking died down, you could hear the busy clicking of the clay weights which held her warp threads taut.

I enjoyed their companionship. With the lamps casting a soft glow around the room and their voices gaily chattering, the fear and the chill that had settled in my heart subsided. The sharp pain receded into a dull ache as gradually the women drew me into their midst, their talk flowing around me like a comforting fire on a cold night. There was a lot to catch up on; it had been a while since I had seen them all together. I didn't travel with them anymore; my joints would ache in the chill night air of the campsites, and the ground had suddenly grown too hard on my bones.

I listened carefully to the tales of my son's miracles coming from the lips of these women. These were His companions, companions to whom the sound of the wind in the date palms, the glow of the stars, and the power of Jesus' presence meant more than the safety of village life. Hearing their stories made me feel young again, and I relived the times when I thrilled to my son's tales of the new Kingdom. I too had tossed my head at the dangers, at my mother's warnings that I should stay home with the others and not wander dirt roads with the other 'rabble', as she had called Jesus' followers.

I had to admit that fishermen, tax collectors, and common sinners could be seen as rabble by my mother, who was quite highborn, but I was young and headstrong, and fear didn't own any corner of my heart. I was with my son, and nothing else mattered.

After Joseph had passed on with an illness, I had more free time, time to spend with Jesus and His followers. I had revelled in the feeling of excitement – the camping, and even the washing of our garments in any river along the way, was fun. I admitted to myself that I missed their companionship.

The evening wore on pleasantly enough, and it was soon time for the women to go back to the camp. Martha and I waved them goodbye, gratefully returning to the warmth of the house. It was time to retire to our beds, but I lay there unable to sleep. I knew that Jesus would have presided over the Passover feast with His twelve disciples, and then they would have made their way to the Mount of Olives.

CHAPTER 25

THE COMPASSIONATE
HEART

J esus loved the Mount of Olives. It was His most favoured
spot each time He was in Jerusalem, and at dusk He could
be found there. He loved the open air; He always felt closer
to His Father out in the open. The crowds always followed
Him everywhere, but at this place He could be alone. Even
His disciples knew not to follow Him when He quietly left
them to have time with His Father. He would go alone up
into the mountains at sunset and would sometimes stay all
night in prayer with His Father. When He returned He was
strengthened, renewed both in His mind and body.

When we first started out along the road, moving from
village to village, I always wondered where the underlying
vigour came from.

When the others wavered in the heat, He would stride
on ahead, His steady pace raising little puffs of dust on the
road, while His disciples, spirits flagging in the heat, would
start to grumble amongst themselves. They were hot and
thirsty; didn't Jesus ever feel the heat and need water?

As if He could sense their anguish from up ahead of
them, He would stop, turn around and smile that wonderful smile of His, which seemed to light up the whole
day. He would point out the shade He had found near a

stream and gently say, 'Come, you are weary, let us rest.'
His followers would meekly follow Him, their grumbling
forgotten – dispersed under the sunshine of His smile.

He was always like that; He understood even the lowli-
est heart. I remembered the way He gently watched Mary
Magdalene as she wiped His feet with her hair. Mary had
spread perfume, very expensive perfume, over His feet.
She wept uncontrollably, and fear filled her heart. She was
a woman with many sins; she came to Him for forgive-
ness and mercy; the effort for her to confront the room
must have been huge. She had entered the dinner without invitation, and the others glared at her. How dare this
fallen woman come into this room? Just look at Jesus, why
doesn't He push her away? Jesus knew their thoughts and,
ignoring them, smiled at the heartbroken woman with
acceptance glowing in His eyes. After she finished her task,
He drew her up to the top of the couch He was lying on and
said to her, 'Your sins have been forgiven; your faith has
saved you. Go in peace.'

He then turned to the host of the dinner and told him
a parable about two men who owed money to a money-
lender. Of the two men, one owed a large amount of money
and the other a smaller amount. As both men in the parable had no money, the money-lender forgave them and
cancelled the debt. Jesus then asked who would love the
money-lender more – the one who owed much or the one
who owed little? Simon, the host of the dinner, chose the
one who owed the most.

Jesus then told Simon that He had entered the dinner,
and no one gave Him water for His feet. No-one gave Him
a kiss of greeting and no-one gave Him oil for His head.

Jesus then pointed out that the woman had anointed Him with perfume, washed His feet with her tears and dried them with her hair. He then said, 'I tell you, her many sins have been forgiven – for she loved much, but he who has been forgiven little, loves little.' That started a wave of whispers and hard stares which, of course, Jesus just ignored.

The woman was now one of His most avid followers. She had turned from her former ways and was living a new life, totally absorbed in Jesus.

Jesus had that ability. When He was in sight, He was like a magnet that drew you to Him. Every sense in your body strained towards Him. To see Him, to hear Him was the only desire that filled your heart. To be blessed by Him, to be the recipient of one of those gentle smiles was Heaven itself.

I thought about that, thought about what Jesus had said: 'My time has come.' Was this wonder to be taken from a thirsty earth? In my heart, I knew that this was so, and the tears once again flowed down my cheeks – selfish tears, tears that were only focused on my own feelings for my son. Even from the time He was twelve years old, He knew that His time on earth was going to be short; He knew that He belonged to the One in Heaven.

There was that time when His brothers and I had gone to see Him where He was preaching. We asked one of the people in the outer ring of the crowd to tell Him we were there and would He please come out to talk with us? We heard His voice saying, 'Who is my mother? Who are my brothers?' Then, pointing to His disciples, He said, 'Look! Here are my mother and my brothers – whoever does what my Father in Heaven wants him to do is my mother and my brothers.'

Yes, even then He belonged to the world – not to me. The ties that held Him to me were cut at that moment. He now belonged to His Father in Heaven, and to the world He had come to save. I could no longer call Him mine, no longer think of Him as the child that grew up in my home or held my hands for support as He started walking; and that awareness broke my heart.

Even so, armed with the knowledge that had just now been revealed to me – that He had said His time had come – I still didn't want Him to leave me. My job of bringing Him into the world, of guiding Him through His childhood years, was now complete, and I mourned for my son. I had believed that His Heavenly Father would leave Him here with for me for a few more years yet. I now realised that my reasons for keeping Him with me were not Heavenly ones, and His Father's reasons for keeping Him to His mission were paramount.

CHAPTER 26

HIS DESTINY CALLS

Quietly, painfully, I accepted what my heart now told me: Jesus' destiny was about to come to pass; His great plan for the redemption of mankind was about to begin. Oh, I had no idea, absolutely no idea what that meant. For now, I was at peace – the transition from mother to one of His disciples had taken place. At last, I had given Him back to His Father; my maternal hold had been broken and I accepted that.

The next few hours passed in a haze, but suddenly there was a pounding of feet and a frantic knocking on Martha's door. I hurriedly got up, wrapped my cloak around me and opened my bedroom door, only to find Martha talking to one of the young men from Jesus' group of followers. He was white and shaking, his face distraught, the tears streaming down his face. Fear struck me dumb, for I recognised him and realised that he had come from Jesus. Words tumbled from trembling lips, accompanied with many sobs. He was becoming incoherent, so Martha gently led him to the kitchen for a drink of water.

At that moment my world crashed in, for the words that were pouring unendingly from him were: 'They have taken Him, they have taken Him,' repeated over and over.

Martha grabbed him by the shoulders and shook him hard; the poor lad hiccupped, wiped his nose and sat silent for a moment. Then he looked up at Martha who asked him sharply, 'Taken who?' The poor lad was beside himself; his next words were the beginning of the end for me, and life would never be the same again. As from the end of a long tunnel, I heard his anguished cry as I fell to my knees.

'Jesus – the soldiers came into the garden, surrounded us all, and then took Him.'

Once again Martha spoke sharply to the young man, who was now weeping wildly, 'How did they find all the disciples, and how did they recognise Jesus? It must have been dark in the garden?'

The young man's face crumpled, eyes red and swollen. I saw the sorrow in them quickly change to anger. 'It was Judas Iscariot, Judas Iscariot! He went up to Jesus and kissed Him. I heard Jesus say, "Judas, is it with a kiss that you betray the Son of Man?" Jesus then turned towards the soldiers and asked them who they were looking for. All the soldiers answered together, "Jesus of Nazareth." Jesus answered, "I am He" – and they all moved back and fell to the ground. Why didn't Jesus run then? He just calmly asked them again, and when they took hold of Him, He said, "If then, you are looking for me, let these others go." Simon Peter attacked the high priest's servant with his sword and cut off his ear. Jesus immediately healed it and told Peter to put up his sword, and then He said something about a cup of suffering His Father had given Him. I didn't understand what Jesus was talking about, but neither did the others, so we all ran like cowards because we were so scared.'

As he spoke, I could hear the shame that he felt. 'We left Him with the soldiers. I do know where they took Him, though. The soldiers were the high priest's guards. I recognised their uniforms, so they must have taken Jesus to Caiaphas' house. He has walked away from them before when He angered them – why not now? Why not tonight? He went willingly with them.' With that, the poor boy sank to the ground at Martha's feet.

I knew now what Jesus had meant when He said, 'My time has come.' Now Jesus' real work was about to begin, the work that His Father had meant Him to do. I could no longer stand, and I sank to my knees in horror.

Martha turned around and saw me on my knees, staring blindly at the door the young man had come through; her face was white with shock. 'Mary,' she said slowly, 'you knew something was going to happen, didn't you? How? How did you know?'

CHAPTER 27

THE PROPHECY
BECOMES CLEAR

I interrupted Martha dully. 'Martha, the prophecy – Simeon's prophecy – and perhaps...' How could I say it was just intuition? I hadn't been given any revelation from Gabriel like I had when Jesus was conceived. No guidance from Joseph, as when we were to go to Egypt right away in the dead of night. I had nothing I could pin my fear on, just an underlying pain in my heart and the knowledge that Jesus' path, His mighty work was about to begin.

Like all the others, I thought His work was here with the world, healing and teaching. Somehow, I could never reconcile the prophecy with His healing and teaching, so I buried it deep, knowing that when the time came, I would know. The part about the spear in my heart didn't make any sense to me then, but now it made perfect sense.

It was only in the hours before young Mark's arrival that I had finally come to terms with the words, 'My time has come,' and then, only since I had been overshadowed by that horrible fortress, did I have this sense of hopelessness, a premonition that my beloved son was in some sort of danger. Now I was swallowed up with fear for my son and a general sense of foreboding. I was beginning to understand my part in Simeon's prophecy, and my heart was finally breaking over the uncertain future of my son.

We sat facing Mark on the couch, waiting for the others. We knew they would be here as soon as they heard the news, and sure enough, within the hour a tentative knock on the door brought our friends and some of the disciples to the house.

They saw me sitting there, my shawl tightly pulled about me, using it like a shield as if the tight cloth would protect me from the pain that was threatening to swamp me. I could see the concern in their eyes. One of the women came across the room and knelt in front of me, 'Oh, Mary, Mary, I am so sorry, please don't cry.' I had not realised that tears were streaming down my face. I looked up and saw Mary Magdalene's concerned face and felt her young arms around my shoulders. She pulled me close, and I gratefully leant against her, at the same time noting that she too was weeping silent tears.

I knew this young woman as the one Jesus had saved from seven demons. Her life had been turned fully around, and now she was fully devoted to Him. He had raised her from a life of scorn and degradation, raised her above the haughty stares, sidelong glances and cruel whispers from the women of Magdala, to the life she now led. The scornful glances had turned into envy, their haughtiness into acceptance; her gratefulness to Him was overwhelming.

CHAPTER 28

THE ARRIVAL OF PETER

The dawn arrived, and with it, another wild knocking at the door. Martha opened the door a crack, expecting soldiers to be there but it was not the soldiers – it was Peter! He burst through the door, nearly knocking Martha over as he rushed in, wild-eyed and dishevelled, words exploding from his tongue as tears streamed down his face. 'I've betrayed Him; I'm cursed!'

We tried to console him, but he was inconsolable. 'He told me that I would deny Him three times before the cock crowed, but I said I would never deny Him. Oh, loathsome man that I am, Jesus knew that I would, and I did!'

Peter continued, 'I was so frightened. I was with John when it happened. He knew one of the high priest's servants, and they let us into the courtyard of the fort. It was so cold that some of the servants had lit a fire and we warmed our hands at the flames. One of the girls said that I was with Jesus; she recognised my accent as Galilean and that I was one of His disciples. I said that I didn't know Him, and then someone else said that, yes I was with Jesus, and another servant around the fire said the same thing. I turned to him and said, "Man, I don't know Him!" – then the rooster crowed three times. I turned around at the noise, just as they brought Jesus out of the high priest's house. He saw me, and the look, the look He gave me. I had betrayed Him! I was as bad as Judas; I betrayed Him when He may have needed me most! I can't live with this. I denied Him, denied Him!' and he collapsed into a shaking, sobbing heap at my feet.

I looked at Peter, dear impulsive Peter, and my heart went out to him. I waited until the tears stopped and, when he was a bit more composed, I asked him, 'Can you tell me what happened, Peter? Tell me slowly and clearly.'

He looked up at me, and the desolation was marked clearly in the lines on his face. 'We were in the garden; we had left the room where we celebrated the Passover and were settling down in our usual place when Jesus decided that He wanted to pray. We were tired. Jesus had been talking to us about many things which we didn't understand. He said something like this: "In a little while you will see Me no more, and then after a while you will see Me again." He could see we were confused and tried to explain. He said, "I tell you the truth. You will weep and mourn while the world rejoices. You will grieve but your grief will turn to joy." We didn't understand; we just didn't understand. What did He mean: "In a little while we will grieve and mourn, and the world will rejoice"?

'Then He asked if we would watch with Him while He went up to pray. Oh, Mary, it had been such a long night, and when He stopped and told us to wait while He went on to pray, we fell asleep!

'We failed Him. We were so sleepy. It was late, and we had just eaten our Passover. The wine and the meal lay heavy upon us.'

I found out much later that Jesus had taken Peter, James and John with Him as He went on to pray, telling the rest of them to wait where they were.

Peter continued, 'Jesus had become very distressed and troubled, and said, "My soul is overwhelmed with sorrow to the point of death. Stay here and keep watch." We went further on with Jesus, who told us to wait while He went to pray to the Father. But the stillness of the night and the light breeze lulled us to sleep.

'We woke guiltily to Jesus' voice saying to us, "Pray lest you fall into temptation." We shook our heads trying to rid ourselves of sleep, with every intention of doing as Jesus asked, but we could not control our sleepiness, and we fell into a deep sleep again. I saw Jesus go on a little further before I fell asleep, and then He fell to the ground praying fervently. It seemed just a minute before He returned and found us sleeping again. Jesus then said, "Simon, are you asleep? Could you not keep watch for just one hour? Watch and pray so that you will not fall into temptation. The spirit is willing, but the body is weak."

'I saw Him go again to pray, and when He returned, we were all sleeping for the third time, so He woke us all, saying, "Are you still sleeping and resting? Look, the Son of Man is betrayed into the hands of sinners. Rise! Let us go! Here comes my betrayer." Then a huge crowd of soldiers came into the garden and headed straight for us. I was terrified. All the guards surrounded us and then Judas, our Judas, came out of the crowd, went up to Jesus and gave Him the kiss of greeting.

'Judas had left our dinner early, and we thought he had gone on an errand for Jesus. Jesus had said that the one who dipped his bread into the bowl with Him would be the one who would betray Him. We all started to ask if it was us and, during the uproar, Jesus spoke quietly to Judas, and he left the room. He must have gone straight to the high priest's house.

'I betrayed Him also – I said I never knew Him! Oh, Mary, He will never forgive me now; I was asleep when He needed company and denied Him when I said I would die for Him.'

He put his head in his hands and started to sob quietly again. I put my hand on his head and said, 'What did you all do next, Peter?'

His look of anguish broke my heart. 'We started to fight the guards, and I cut off the ear of one of the high priest's servants, but Jesus told me to put down my sword, and He healed the servant's ear. He then said, "Do you think that I cannot call on my Father and He will at once put at my disposal more than twelve legions of angels? How then would the scriptures be fulfilled that say it must happen this way?"'

I heard Peter's voice, but my mind was back with Simeon's prophecy, and I knew without a doubt that this was Jesus' work. He was going to die, for what I still didn't know, but I was sure that this was to be my beloved son's end. I shook my head, bringing my mind back to Peter, who was still telling his story.

'It was strange,' said Peter. 'When Jesus asked them who they wanted, He said, "I am He," and all the soldiers fell down. The strange thing was, He didn't run. He just waited for them to get up and then He asked them again who they wanted. I tried to protect Him, but He went willingly, quietly.'

Poor impetuous Peter, I thought. He didn't understand, but then neither did I... until just a while ago. Jesus was going about His Father's business as He always did, quietly, obediently and with little fuss. I heaved a great sigh. There were no more tears left to cry at present.

Peter continued with his story: 'I followed after them carefully; it was easy really, the soldiers were marching quickly, in a hurry to get to the place they were taking Jesus, and no-one bothered to check the few people who were following after them. We got to the house of Caiaphas.'

Here I interrupted, 'We? Who else was with you, Peter?'

'Oh,' said Peter, 'It was young John.' John Mark, the young man who had burst in with the first telling of this dreadful episode. Peter continued, 'John knew one of Caiaphas' servant girls, and they let him in, and then a bit later, they opened the door and let me in too. One of the servant girls saw me and questioned me, and she asked if I was one of Jesus' disciples. I said I wasn't.' Peter shot me a glance and said, 'Mary, I was so frightened.'

I soothed his brow. 'Hush, what next, Peter?'

CHAPTER 29

PETER'S BETRAYAL

With a sorrowful look, Peter took a deep breath and continued his story. 'Well, it was so cold that I walked over to the fire to warm myself, and then someone else asked me if I was a disciple. I said no again, and then someone else took my arm and said, "Haven't I seen you before at the olive grove with Jesus and the rest of His disciples?" I was so terrified that I said, "No, I don't know the man!" – and then the cock crowed... just like He said it would.'

'Peter,' I shook his arm. He was staring in mute agony into the flames of the fire Martha had built up against the cold. 'Peter, what do you mean, just like He said it would? Peter...' He looked up at me, and I saw the depths of his anguish as he began to answer me. 'Jesus told me that I would deny Him three times before the cock crowed... and I did.'

'Peter, I don't understand what you are saying,' I said.

Peter spoke slowly to me, 'It was when we were at the feast in the upper room. Jesus was telling us that He was going to leave us, and He said, "Where I am going you cannot come," and then He told us to love one another as He had loved us. I asked Him where He was going, and He said, "Where I am going you cannot follow" – but that I would follow later. I asked Him why I could not follow, as I would lay down my life for Him.' A sob broke from Peter's trembling lips and his eyes filled with tears.

'He knew I would deny Him even then because He said, "Before the rooster crows you will disown Me three times." And I did. Oh, Mary, I did just that to save my own miserable skin! I saw Him before they took Him away – He turned towards me, and Mary, His face was so bruised, but it was the sadness in the way He was looking at me – I can still see it. I betrayed Him not once, but three times! I denied my Lord. Will He ever forgive me? Oh, Mary, I am lost!'

'What then, Peter?' I asked.

'Well, after I saw Jesus... Oh, Mary, His hands were bound like a common criminal... after He looked at me, I was so ashamed that I just raced out of the gate and came back here. Oh, Mary, what am I going to do? He will never forgive me now.'

I looked at the distraught man at my feet, tear-stained, dishevelled, wild-eyed and desperate. What could I say to him that would ease his pain? – when my own pain threatened to overwhelm me. We just sat together, bound in mutual pain for the one who was the dearest to us in the whole world – one of us His disciple, the other His mother. We both started praying together; I am not sure what Peter was praying for. I was praying not for His release, but for the strength He would need to carry out His God-given task.

Martha had been standing nearby, and she bent down and lifted Peter to his feet. 'Come, Peter, you need to rest. I have a hot drink here for you,' and she handed him a cup. 'Have you eaten? I know you shared in the Passover, but it is nearly morning now, nearly time for you to break your fast.' Peter started to protest, but Martha, dear practical Martha never, ever tolerated any nonsense, and she quietly guided Peter into another room.

The night wore on, and daylight filtered through the window; very soon, the sounds of other households waking to the rays of the sun filled the empty room. Martha's house overlooked the street, and we could hear people going to the synagogue for morning prayer. I heard the baker calling out his wares, and children's laughter. The world still carried on as before – our tragedy was not yet the world's; no-one knew but the disciples and those who were at Martha's home.

A little later, Martha brought us some dates and bread for breakfast, insisting that we ate. She was always sensible, always concerned... 'Mary, eat – you're going to need the strength that food will give you.'

By the time we had finished eating, we could no longer ignore the commotion outside. Snatches of conversation could be heard through the now open window. 'Hey, did you know that Jesus has been arrested?' said one man. 'I think He is at the fortress,' said another. People were now streaming up the street beneath our window. Amongst the sounds of running feet, more shouts could be heard – 'They've taken Him to Herod,' floated up through the window. The words that hurt the most were: 'Do you think He's guilty of what they are accusing Him of?' I never heard the answer to that – I placed my hands over my ears and thought, 'How could they even think He was guilty of anything?'

I sat quite still, unable to trust my legs to hold me. Martha came over to where I was sitting with a hot drink for me. 'Come, Mary, drink this and then we will go to the high priest's house and see what we can find out about Jesus.'

CHAPTER 30

I MUST GO TO HIM

'Thank you, Martha,' I said. 'I have to go to Him; I must be near Him. I know I cannot do anything, but as His mother, I might be allowed to see Him.' I looked at Martha, 'Wouldn't they? I am His mother, after all.' The look on her face told me that no, they would not let me see Him.

The others had left earlier but we had stayed back on the chance that they might release Him, or the others might have news and need to find us urgently.

Martha placed her arm about my shoulders and helped me to stand. I was so grateful for her concern. My world had suddenly become too much to bear, and I couldn't think about what I should do. I wanted to be with my son but had no idea how that could happen. Would we, as His followers, be arrested also?

I was so confused. I knew that I should stay where I was just in case news came that He had been released, but my legs walked me unbidden to the door. As I neared it, Martha's kindly voice floated somewhere nearby, and I felt her put my shawl about my shoulders. 'You will need this, Mary. We will wait no longer. It's nearly mid-morning, let's go.'

I pulled open the door and saw the crowd seething like a

torrent past the foot of the steps; here and there islands of colour floated, as the veils and head baskets of fruit drifted past. The noise hit me like a physical blow, and I detected the crowd's mood to be more sinister than usual.

A crowded street was usual near Martha's home, and most of the time, the noise of the people was joyous and excited. Today, however, I could see the faces of the men in the crowd, and they were not jubilant. Anger was flaring, as groups of people argued. These groups were like flotsam being pushed along, and I could feel a tangible sense of hatred emanating from this tumbling river of humanity; my fear grew to immense proportions.

'Martha, I hope we're not too late! Oh, let's hurry!'

I stepped out into the stream of humanity and almost fell under a violent shove when I stepped in front of a man. 'Here! Watch where you're going – get out of my way, woman!' he muttered rudely as he and his friend pushed past.

'Hope we're not too late,' the man said. 'I heard they found Him guilty.' This last sentence was more than I could bear, and I grabbed his arm.

'Who? Who have they found guilty?'

The man shook my hand off. 'Jesus – that's who! Are you one of the rabble that follow Him? Good job, that's what I say – you're nothing but a lot of troublemakers and that Jesus is the worst of the lot!' With that he turned away, but a minute later he turned around again and said, 'If you're one of them, I'd watch out, woman – it's a dark day for the lot of you, you mark my words.' With those fearful words, he turned and plunged after his mate, and was lost in the crowd.

Martha's face was as white as mine must have been.

'Martha, it's too late,' I said. 'Hurry! We must get to the fortress; that's where they must have Him.'

However, this was easier said than done – the streets were narrow and heavily paved. Houses opened onto the streets, and their steps created an obstacle, causing blockages as people clambered over or around them any way they could, just to keep moving. Martha and I joined this river of crazy humanity and could do nothing but go with it, hoping perhaps to find a side street leading away from this mayhem and over to the fortress.

We thought that perhaps this crowd might have been going to the Temple, but no – they turned into the street leading down to the fortress ahead of me, as I too clambered over yet another set of steps.

CHAPTER 31

BEFORE PILATE

Finally, I saw the fortress. This was the place where I had bumped into the guard when I first arrived, and it was the place where that terrible foreboding came over me. I dreaded going over there but knew that if I wanted to know anything about my son, I needed to go.

To get to the fortress, we had to fight our way through the crowds that surrounded it. Jerusalem was bursting at the seams, and the whole place was awash with people crowding around the base of the fortress. Above their heads, the Roman governor, Pontius Pilate, was calling down to the chief priests arrayed below him. I was near enough to see clearly, but not to hear what he was saying. I did, however, hear the chanting which swelled like a great wind and burst upon my ears.

'Barabbas! Barabbas!' I couldn't believe my ears. I asked someone near me who Barabbas was, and he informed me that he was a rebel leader who had been captured some time ago and had been charged with murder.

'Where have you been lady,' the man said, 'that you don't know what's been happening?'

I breathed a sigh of relief; he hadn't asked who I was or warned me to run if I belonged to Jesus' group of disciples.

'I'm from the country,' I answered.

'Well,' he said, 'the high priest has arrested that rabble-rouser Jesus and accused Him of blasphemy.'

I interrupted, 'Blasphemy! Surely not, why would they do that?'

The man turned away for a minute, looking up at the balcony as another roar came from the crowd. 'They said He called Himself the Son of God. Now, lady, do you mind, I'm busy.' He turned away and, pushing through the crowd to get a better view of the balcony, he disappeared from sight.

Looking up at the balcony, I saw that Pilate had gone inside again. 'Martha, maybe Jesus will be okay. They are all calling for Barabbas.'

'Yes, I heard,' she smiled ruefully. Martha started to say something else, but the crowd's mood changed, and an eerie silence settled over them for a moment. I strained up to see if I could see what was happening, and realised that Pilate was back on the balcony. I could see that he was saying something – something the crowd didn't like because their disapproval was sharp and constant.

Once again, I couldn't hear or see what was happening through the seething mass of humanity. Looking around in despair, I suddenly saw the soldiers of the high priest worming their way into the crowd from around the fringes, positioning themselves near the middle of the people. I was now beyond curiosity, and frantic to get closer to the fortress so that I could hear what Pilate was saying. Losing all sense of dignity, I let go of Martha's hand and plunged into the crowd, shoving and ducking, ignoring the catcalls and anger as I took every advantage of gaps in the crowd to get closer, desperate to hear what was happening. As soon as I let go of her hand, Martha followed me. She was a little bit larger than me, and the men gave way in front of her quite easily. The look on her face stopped any hassles and, reaching me, she grabbed my hand as we wove our way closer to the wall.

CHAPTER 32

BARABBAS

After we reached the wall, Martha turned to me and said, 'Mary, oh, Mary! We shouldn't have come.' She put her arms around me, her face stained with tears. I stared dumbly at her.

'No, Martha, I need to know. Hush, Pilate is on the balcony again.'

Pilate knew that it was out of envy that the chief priests had handed Jesus over to him. 'Do you want me to release to you the king of the Jews?' he said.

I couldn't believe my ears because – next thing – the soldiers of the high priest were pushing their way into the centre of the crowd shouting, 'Barabbas!' Then the crowd followed, also shouting 'Barabbas!' Just like the sheep that they were – no minds of their own, no thought to look and see if this was justice or not. If the Pharisees say this, then it must be right and true, and we will follow them. Sheep! I was devastated.

The chanting continued as Pilate turned towards the crowd, who were calling out to him, 'Give us a choice like you usually do!'

Pilate took a step back and, looking behind him, saw one of the soldiers trying to get his attention. He spoke with the soldier for a moment, read the note that was handed to him then came forward and asked the high priest a question.

My heart sank. Why is Pilate listening to the crowd? Surely, he knew what they wanted. Surely he knew the twisted minds of men like Caiaphas only wanted one thing, the death of my son.

The high priest's soldiers began stirring up the crowd, 'Barabbas! Barabbas!' they chanted, and soon the whole crowd was calling for Barabbas. The world made no sense to me anymore. The crowd was full of men and women who had been healed by my son, had listened to His sermons, had followed Him, and now were calling for His death. Had the world had gone mad?

Pilate wanted to release Jesus, so he appealed to the crowd again, but now they were shouting, 'Crucify Him! Crucify Him!'

Pilate waved them to silence and spoke to them again. 'Why? What crime has He committed? I have found in Him no grounds for the death penalty. Therefore, I will punish Him and then release Him.'

Now the shouts grew louder; they demanded that Jesus be crucified, so Pilate turned and called for a bowl of water. After it was brought to him, he turned to the crowd and, washing his hands in the bowl, said: 'I am innocent of this man's blood – you crucify Him!'

What I heard next astonished me, for all the people answered, 'Let His blood be on us and on our children.'

Pilate turned to the soldier behind him and said, 'Release Barabbas.'

Did the crowd know what they were saying? These were our priests – the men who were supposed to be our shepherds, but they were now showing their true light. They were wolves; wolves that let the sheep they were supposed to be protecting fall into a deadly trap.

The tears began to flow again, and Martha turned to me, her face also stained with tears. 'Mary, did you hear what is going to happen to Jesus?' I stared dumbly at her; her voice seemed to be coming from a long way off. I shook my head, trying to shake off the numbness, trying with all my might to concentrate. I only knew something was happening, because the crowd was moving away from the balcony and crowding around the gate to the fortress.

But something more sinister was going on. From where Martha and I were standing near the wall I could hear the sounds of soldiers having fun with a prisoner – mocking him, spitting and laughing scornfully. Then I heard the sounds of a whip, the cracking sound and dull thud it made as it landed on the back of the poor prisoner they had been mocking. The sound curdled my stomach, and I gagged but managed to stay in control.

The sound seemed to go on for ages. It was strange though, that all I heard was the grunting of the soldiers who I thought must have been wielding the whip. I had heard tales of that whip, and my mind was whirling. What dreadful thing had that prisoner done to be subjected to such horrific treatment? I wanted to get away – the Romans were cruel, and we knew they used this method to control the populace. Their use of fear kept the peace but won them no friends.

CHAPTER 33

THE WAY TO
THE CROSS

I saw that soldiers had started to march through the gate. Just in front of them was a man carrying a heavy bar of wood. I could see this man bend under the lash of the whip; then there was another soldier, followed by a second figure. It was this man that drew my eyes as He stumbled under the weight of the wood. His garment was stained with blood; on His head was what looked like a crown.

Then I heard Martha's cry of anguish. 'It's Jesus!' she said.

I gasped in horror, 'No, no! They couldn't, surely they wouldn't!' I couldn't believe the brutality that had been levelled against my beloved son. I suddenly realised that the prisoner I had heard being mocked and spat on was Jesus, and they were using that brutal whip on him – the one they used before crucifixion... crucifixion! I let out another cry, and Martha turned to me, squeezing my hand tightly as we watched my son walk out of the fortress.

Jesus wore a robe around His shoulders; I thought it might be a royal robe, one that a king might wear. It was heavily stained, but I could see the purple around its edges, and what was that on His head? I knew what wreaths looked like. I had seen them on Pilate's head, but this one was very different – it was pushed down on His head, almost to His eyebrows, and it looked as if it was full of thorns.

Why would a loving God put His Son through such horror and such pain? I thought my son was to be the Saviour of His people. How could this – this horror – save His people? How could the Pharisees have twisted and used Pilate to get rid of Jesus? My thoughts caused me to stumble, and I gratefully took hold of Martha's arm. Was this His Father's work – crucifixion? How could that be of any use? I railed in my mind at the Father, while all the time trying to get closer to my son.

My thoughts turned back to Simeon's prophecy. What he said then didn't make any sense but, now that I understood, my heart felt as though a spear had entered it, tearing it apart.

The third soldier came through the gate, followed by another man, and the gate closed.

The appalling caravan started to wind its way through the street. The crowd parted but was not silent. Shouts and wailing filled the air: the men's hurled shouts of jubilation, the women's tears and screams of unbelief.

My son's name echoed through the street, and He turned and spoke to some of the women who were standing close by. I was so appalled that my son's last words were given to others, not to me – I couldn't get close enough even to see Him. The unfairness of it stung badly.

Then I heard a sigh go through the crowd and heard the whip come down on the back of one of the prisoners. The soldier was whipping the prisoner who had dropped the bar He was carrying. Standing on tiptoe, I saw with horror that it was my son who had dropped His bar, and the soldier was furiously beating Him trying to make Him rise. My heart broke; the ache was so intense. My whole universe had shrunk to this sharp piercing pain that ripped through my body. From far away, I thought that this was rather like giving birth, but how could I be giving birth when my son was going to die?

Slowly, I came to my senses, just as my son stumbled again as He was trying to rise. I saw a woman rush forward with her water jar to give Him a drink. I also rushed towards Him through the crowd, pushing and shoving at the people in my way. A cruel blow from a soldier spun me around, and I could only watch painfully as my son, using the ends of the bar for leverage, tried to push Himself up on His feet. He stood up and started to shuffle forward, His face a mass of livid bruises. His tunic at the back was soaked with His blood, and He was bleeding freely from every one of His numerous wounds – yet the soldiers still cursed and prodded at Him with the handles of their whips.

I had to go to Him, to let Him know I was there. Some of the priests had tired of the excruciating game of inciting the people and, with their absence, spaces appeared in the crowd. I took advantage of them, pushing people aside, ignoring their complaints. I leaned out into the road, standing as far out as I could; I needed to see my son's face, to let Him know that I was near.

I held my breath. Yes, I could see Him now, but I could also see that He had fallen once again. I cried out, 'Can't you see He is too weak? He has lost too much blood!' Still the soldier raised his whip, bringing it down hard on my son's back. He valiantly tried to rise, but it was just too much. He sank down again and the bar He was trying to lift fell to the ground once more.

I cried out His name. I had managed to get close. Martha had followed, but her bulk had made her slower than me. Just as she arrived, Jesus looked up and saw me. The sadness in His eyes was just too much. I was grateful for Martha's arm around my shoulders. I did not want my son to see the effect that all of this was having on me. I must be there for Him – strong, not weak and ineffective. This was Simeon's prophecy; my pain was the result of my son's pain.

Even with Martha's arm around my shoulder, I was unsteady on my feet, trying to see what was happening through the gaps in the crowd, trying not to weep.

Suddenly I was roughly pushed aside by a centurion who was pointing to someone behind me. 'You! Pick up the bar the prisoner dropped. Carry it for Him!'

The man was reluctant to move but soon changed his mind when the centurion lifted his whip to enforce his command. We found out later that the man was called Simon. He bent and picked up the bar, and my son lifted His face to thank him, only to be forcibly dragged to His feet and made to walk ahead. Was it my imagination, or did a look pass between the man and my son? Because the angry look faded from the countenance of the man, and he picked up the bar, following the faltering steps of Jesus down the street to the gate.

The weeping and wailing by the women who followed this sad procession caused my son to turn and speak with them, but I was a little way away and could not hear His words. I could only see the compassion on His face; compassion for the women who were following when His own life was draining away. Only my son could have done such a thing.

The sad procession halted a few more times as my son stumbled. The crowd felt no pity – their tormenting, their cursing and their laughter continued. I followed Him, struggling to keep up, struggling with the hate that was like a dark cloud surrounding us, while also struggling to keep Martha in my sight. We had been separated by the surging throng of people as they all fought to get out of Jerusalem and up the path to Golgotha, where they were taking my son.

CHAPTER 34

GOLGOTHA

Finally I passed through the gates of Jerusalem – was it really only yesterday that I came through these very same gates, hoping to see Jesus? So much had happened since then. It felt as though I had aged ten years in as many moments; I wondered if I would ever be the same again. This was definitely not the procession I had ever thought I would join.

I had skirted funeral processions many times before. Death was commonplace at this time of the year. Famine was always just around the corner. Life was hard; if the seasons were unkind to us, death haunted our footsteps. Food could be scarce if rain didn't come. The old, the sick, and sometimes the very young would succumb to its icy fingers, so death was something we were not afraid of – but this...

With my thoughts elsewhere, I struck my foot against a rock, and the resulting pain brought my thoughts back to the present. 'Mary, you're rambling,' I said to myself. 'I've gone mad,' I thought.

The path rounded a bend then followed the contours of the hill, reaching a huge rock which stood in the way. It then split into two separate tracks – one going up to the top where the soldiers were now heading, and another that went to a spot a little below and to the side. This was where the main throng wound up, not wanting to be near while the soldiers carried out their grisly task.

I rested against the rock, trying to see Martha. I had lost her completely now. Only the few people who pushed ahead up the track were in sight. Somehow I didn't care; I didn't want her pity. Her grief was as overwhelming as mine and, try as I might, I couldn't bear the thought of her loving concern. My grief was so all-encompassing that everything else faded into insignificance beside it.

The soldiers must have reached the top because I could hear the harsh command of the centurions. I placed my hands over my ears at the sounds of the hammers against the nails, and the awful cries of the prisoners ringing out. I was glad I had not followed up to the top with those who had gathered there. I knew that hearing the cries of my son would be too much. I wanted to be there, wanted to share in His last moments, but the pain in my heart held me where I was, stationary behind the large rock at the division of the paths rising up to the brow of the hill.

I never dreamt that it would be like this. This was... I couldn't think anymore. I had no more tears, just an irrational thought that this was a nightmare that I would wake from shortly. I heard the shouts as the centurions threaded the ropes through the rings on the arms of the crosses, ready to hoist the prisoners into the air, and waited for the sound of the crosses dropping into their holes.

So much crying and screaming was going on all around me that I did not hear the footsteps that were coming towards me. Suddenly an arm went around my shoulders, and I jumped.

CHAPTER 35

JOHN WHOM
JESUS LOVED

Turning around, I saw that the man who had put his arm around me was John. Dear John – how my son loved this fresh-faced young man. Normally his eyes were clear, and he always seemed to be looking on horizons we lesser humans could not see. He was quietly-spoken, loving and gentle, yet he possessed in the depths of his being a strong, steady belief that Jesus was the Son of God. He knew that one day Jesus would bring about His glorious Kingdom, just as the Scriptures and my son said.

I was very fond of John and, looking at the young man as he turned to me, I saw his face was swollen from the tears that flowed down his cheeks. I so wanted to gather him in my arms. He was like a little lost lamb, and I couldn't make up my mind who needed comfort the most.

'Mary, oh my poor Mary, let me take you back. You can do no good here.'

I shook my head. 'No, John, I must go to Him one more time.' With that I turned, wrapped my shawl once more about me and determinedly started walking up the same path my son had just climbed to His death, up the path to Golgotha.

I had seen the chief priests take the path leading to the

plateau, followed by the Sadducees and the soldiers, and I could hear their voices – voices filled with hate, hurling insults at my son. I looked down upon them and felt such shame; these were Israel's priests, the leaders of our people. Yet, standing there in a group, with their gorgeous robes billowing in the wind, they looked like great birds of prey.

The wind had begun to blow hard. On the horizon, I detected black clouds which were dark and ominous. I could hear the venom-filled voices of the priests from where I was standing; there was no stopping their hatred. I heard one priest yell, 'He saved others, let Him save Himself if He is the Messiah!' It took all my strength not to run down the path and onto the plateau; I was grateful for the restraining arm around my shoulders.

'Mary, Mary, leave them – they are not worth your anger, leave them be. A higher power than yours or mine will extract the payment due to them. Let us continue on our journey.'

I knew John was right and looked up into his calm face; he had gathered the strength to stop his tears and had wiped his face dry.

As I thought about the priests, I remembered something Jesus had said. He mentioned that their father was the father of lies. At that time, I don't think I followed what He was saying. A lot of what my son said went over my head, but this stuck in my mind. Who was the father of lies? Looking at the priests now, I didn't need to be told who their father was. I could see quite clearly that they were completing a task, a task given to them by a higher master. They were puppets, and their master was pulling the strings. How he was laughing. He had done it! The Son of God was crucified. His objective had been accomplished – but had it?

Looking around, it appeared so, but I couldn't help thinking, 'This can't be all there is, it can't be. This is the Son of God; Satan couldn't possibly win over God. Could he?'

Turning away from their yelling, John and I walked over the crest of the hill. Three crosses stood starkly against an increasingly darkening sky. My eyes took in the horrific scene; saw painfully what they had done to my son. We stood near the execution site; the soldiers did not push us back, being far too busy to bother about a few peasants.

CHAPTER 36

CRUCIFIED

I could now see the brutality with which they had treated my son, my child. When I saw Him outside the fortress, His tunic hid what I could now plainly see. They had stripped Him bare, and to the right of His cross I could see the soldiers gambling for His clothes. This was the final humiliation – He was spread bare for all to look upon – that is, if you could see through the blood that was smeared on His still-bleeding body.

I was beyond feeling anything now. I just wanted to get to His cross, to let Him know I was there.

The man on one of the crosses was calling out, struggling against the nails and hurling curses at my son. The other was just watching quietly, and then he strained against the nails and said, 'Don't you fear God, since you are under the same sentence? We are punished justly, for we are getting what our sins deserved, but this man has done no wrong.' He then looked at Jesus and said, 'Jesus, remember me when you come into your Kingdom.'

The quiet words of the criminal fell on the ears of Jesus, who slowly turned His head and looked upon the man dying beside Him. He saw all the sad life that had brought the criminal finally here to this cruel cross. Jesus watched as belief dawned in the criminal's eyes and the shadow of death began drawing in. Jesus then answered him, 'I tell you the truth, today you will be with me in paradise.'

I looked hard at my son. He was on the middle cross, His head bowed. The blood from the nails in His hands trickled slowly down from the crossbar, dripping in a steady trail onto the ground. I gasped at the state of His poor body; the soldiers had certainly done a thorough job with their cruel whip. I could find no part of His body that was not torn open. His forehead, which bore that monstrous crown of thorns, had stopped trickling blood, and all one could see were the tracks that it had made down His cheeks. He was having difficulty breathing, and I watched as He pulled Himself up from the nails to catch a breath.

As I took all this in, a soldier pushed past me and, laying a ladder against my son's cross, climbed up to nail a sign above His head. I strained to read what it said and could just make out the words written in Latin, Aramaic and Greek: 'Jesus of Nazareth, the King of the Jews.'

The priests howled – they didn't like it at all and raced off down the hill. I wondered where they were going. Later, I found out that they had gone to Pilate, telling him to change the sign to: 'This man claimed to be the King of the Jews,' but Pilate refused, saying, 'What I have written stays written.'

I looked up at John. 'We must draw closer, John – I must be near Him. He must see me, know that I am near. I was there at the beginning, and I will be there at His end, no matter how terrifying it is.'

John's face fell, his heart already breaking from the sight

of the pain on his master's face, for the indignities forced upon Him and the stripes on His body that bore witness to the terrible scourging He had received. As we got closer, we could see yet another indignity heaped upon Him – not by the Romans, but by the Jews themselves. There were bloody, bald patches in His beard. To pull out a person's beard was the highest insult; it showed disrespect and contempt.

John looked at me and faltered. Later, he told me about the mess I was in; my tears had left tracks in the dust on my face, a face that was grey with fatigue and aged with grief. Before he could say anything though, I was gone. I slipped easily from his grasp, hurried through the jeering people and fell to my knees in front of the cross. John followed and heard my anguished cry, 'Son, oh my son! Oh, that I could have spared you this!'

Jesus opened the eye that was not so horrendously swollen as He heard my voice – heard it above the crowd, heard it as He had in His childhood and knew it was me, His mother, knew it was the place of safety. He also saw John, His beloved cousin, son of Salome, the disciple that he loved. Struggling for breath, He spoke to me saying, 'Dear woman, here is your son,' and then to John, 'Here is your mother.'

I very nearly collapsed at those words. Even so near to His death, my son, my dearest son's thoughts were for me and my welfare. The tears flowed again. I had thought that I would never have enough tears to cry ever again, but the well had not yet run dry.

As we were speaking with Jesus, the centurion who had nailed the sign above Jesus' head reached for a sponge and, dipping it in a bucket, placed the sponge on to a hyssop stalk and lifted it to Jesus' lips. The centurion looked at me and said, 'He said He was thirsty.'

Jesus received the drink, then in a loud voice cried, 'It is finished!' His head dropped to His chest, and He died.

The centurion, who handed up the hyssop for Jesus, hearing His cry and seeing how He died, said in wonder, 'Surely this was the Son of God!'

Until this moment I had felt completely numb but now, as my son breathed His last, a great wave of sorrow pushed me to my knees and tears of grief finally broke loose. All thoughts of staying strong – to not show my pain in case it frightened young John – vanished, as the sobs that reached to the bottom of my soul overwhelmed me. John's arms came around my shoulders as he gently lifted me to my feet and turned me away. Slowly we walked towards some of our women who were watching from a distance. Among them were Mary Magdalene and Mary, the mother of James, and Salome. These women followed Jesus and His disciples, but there were many other women there also who all followed my son.

CHAPTER 37

NATURE MOURNS

The wailing from our women was terrible to hear, but something more terrifying was happening. The dark cloud that had been drawing nearer and nearer had finally reached Golgotha. The light disappeared, the day became like midnight, and then the earth began to shake violently. People started running in all directions, and chaos of a different kind now reigned.

People were being trampled and knocked off their feet as the pathway up to Golgotha was not very wide. Two or three could walk comfortably together along it, but not the number of people who were now trying to run down the path. The shaking earth did nothing to help people keep their feet. John and I, with the other women, waited until the stampede had gone before we too descended to flat ground and headed for Martha's house.

Martha! I had forgotten about her. Where was she? I searched the faces of those who were still running past me but could not find her. John thought she must have returned home long ago. We both knew she didn't like heights or crowds of people around her, so it made sense that when she lost me, she may have turned around and gone back to her home. She would be waiting for us there.

This thought kept going through my head – 'What is going to happen to us all without my beloved son?' Then all I could think about was the desperate state of my son's body. How could He have taken all that punishment, yet still be the gentle soul I knew? I had heard that nothing came from His lips in all the time He was in the hands of those dreadful soldiers. He also remained silent on the balcony, even when the crowd was baying for His blood. He did not try to defend Himself before Pilate and, even when they released Barabbas, He did not utter a word. This was the Father's will, and He was obedient to it.

For all of us, His followers, the danger was very real. We were all frightened, knowing full well the Pharisees would not stop with my son. All of us were now in very real danger, but even though He had taken care of my welfare, I was concerned for His little band. I knew that the priests thought that by killing Him, they had forever stopped His band of followers; but to make sure, they would hunt us all down until not one of us was left. This thought caused me trouble. Would all His work be for nothing?

When we got back to Martha's house, we found most of the disciples there, all talking at once. Every time there was a knock at the door, their faces told the fear they all felt. With each knock, we looked at one another until one brave soul got up and opened the door to yet another of my son's followers. A huge sigh of relief passed around the room – it was not a soldier – and all the talk started again.

CHAPTER 38

A RICH MAN'S
TOMB

I heard later that Joseph of Arimathea, a rich disciple and a member of the Sanhedrin, had not had anything to do with Jesus' arrest. He went to Pilate to ask for Jesus' body. All the disciples had been so afraid that they ran away. It was left to others to provide for Jesus' burial. You had to have Pilate's approval before you could take bodies down from their crosses; a precaution against relatives or friends taking down the bodies and reviving them.

Pilate agreed, and Joseph, with the help of Nicodemus (the man who had visited Jesus at night), took my son's body to Joseph's own tomb, which had just been hewn out of the rock in preparation for his own death. After they had cleaned the blood from His body, Nicodemus applied the special spices, which was our custom in the burial of the dead. The two men then laid Him to rest. It was our Day of Preparation – the sun had nearly set, and Sabbath was the next day when no work was to be done.

This was the night I could not sleep and had got up, finally finding my way to the place where I was now sitting. I sat up and saw it was nearly morning; time had gone by so quickly that the birds had begun to sing, and the sun was starting to light the tops of the trees. I stood up, ready to walk back to Martha's house.

When I arrived, Martha was looking quite worried. 'Mary, you're here! We went to wake you, but your room was empty.'

'I couldn't sleep,' I said, 'so I got up and went for a walk; I sat leaning against a tree and must have dropped off. I hope I didn't scare you.'

CHAPTER 39

AN EMPTY TOMB

M artha shook her head. 'Mary, we were worried about you. You should have woken one of the men, and they would have walked with you. I have some news for you; we don't know what has happened, but Mary Magdalene went to the tomb this morning quite early and came running back saying the tomb was empty.'

I couldn't understand what she was saying. 'What do you mean the tomb was empty? I saw them lay Jesus into it.'

'Yes, I know, but it was empty,' Martha said. 'Peter and John went with her to check it out and saw it was empty. John just looked in and saw the strips of linen lying there but did not go in. Then Peter, who was running behind him, arrived and went into the tomb for a look. He also saw the strips of linen as well as the head cloth that had been around Jesus' head. The cloth was folded up by itself, separate from the linen. Finally, John went back in again for another look. Something Jesus had said to them went through his mind: "You will see me no more and after a while you will see me again..." He still did not fully under-stand the meaning of the empty tomb. He was bewildered, but he felt a strange sense of hope. They came back and reported that Mary was right, then returned to their homes.'

I must have looked shocked. Martha put her hand on my arm and said, 'Mary, there is more – He has risen.'

'Risen?' I said.

'Yes, risen.' Martha carried on. 'I told you that Mary Magdalene went first to the tomb, then came back and told Peter and John. She went back with them but stayed at the tomb after they left. She says that, as she was crying at the tomb, she bent over to look into the tomb and saw two angels in white sitting where Jesus had been laid – one at the head and the other at the foot.'

CHAPTER 40

THE GARDENER

The angels had asked Mary Magdalene why she was crying. She told them that someone had taken away her Lord, and she didn't know where they had put Him. As she was speaking to them, she turned around and saw a man standing there. The man also asked her why she was crying, and who it was she was looking for.

Thinking He was the gardener, she said, 'If you have carried Him away, tell me where you have put Him, and I will get Him.'

'Well,' Martha continued the story, 'the man called her by her name, and she then recognised Him. It was Jesus! He said to her, "Do not hold onto me for I have not yet returned to the Father. Go instead to my brothers and tell them that I am returning to my Father and your Father, to my God and your God."'

Mary had gone immediately to the disciples with the news: 'I have seen the Lord,' and she told them that He had said these things to her.

My heart skipped a beat. 'Jesus alive? – it can't be!'

'Yes, it can, Mary! Remember He told us that He would come to us after a little while? Remember that He said, "In a little while you will not see me and the world will rejoice, and then you will see me." None of us understood at that time but, Mary, He has risen! He is our God!'

I sat down fast – Risen! Our God! 'Oh...' and the tears flowed again.

CHAPTER 41

JOY, REALISATION AND ACCEPTANCE

'My son is alive,' and then I suddenly realised that God's Son lived!

This whole revelation was just too much for me at that time. The separation was complete. I bore Him, taught Him and cared for Him in His formative years, but now I truly saw Him as God's Son – and my heart ached at this. Yet, joy filled my heart at the magnificent ways of the Father. I would once more see Jesus, not just as my son, but as God's Son too. How would I feel when I saw Him again?

I chided myself, 'Mary, what are you thinking? He will always be your firstborn. Now, pull yourself together. Think! He is no longer dead; He has risen!' Joy filled my heart, the pain receded, and the dreadful time of His death melted into joy at His return to life – I would see Him once again!

On the evening of the first day, when we were all together with the doors locked for fear of the Jews, Jesus came and stood among us. I would like to try to explain to you the joy that filled me to overflowing. The first thing I noticed was the wonderful fragrance that filled the room, the warmth and sense of safety – all our fears were gone. We were not afraid of the Jews anymore. Jesus showed us His hands and the side that the centurion had pierced, proving that it was really Him. Then He said, 'Peace be with you.'

I can tell you, when He looked around at me, my heart overflowed. He did recognise me! He was still approachable, still my son, only now – and I truly understood this – He belonged to us all. He was our God, our Saviour – the Son who from now on would represent us before our Father's throne.

His presence warmed our hearts; we loved Him and now we knew how much He loved us. How blessed we were to have lived beside Him, to have been His friends. I thanked the Father for the journey He had taken me on.

After Jesus had left us, once again through the locked door, I sat thinking about what I have been telling you now. I thought of Simeon's prophecy – Jesus had caused the falling and rising of many in Israel. He was spoken against, and the thoughts of many hearts had been revealed. I thought of His death, how He had been hunted and tricked, and how the priests had shown their true feelings at the cross.

I remembered at His birth how a king had been so scared of Him that he had murdered all the male children under two years old in a whole village. I thought of their mothers' pain, while I had escaped with my son.

I thought about the three wise men and their gifts, which helped us to live in Egypt. I also thought of all the pain that Simeon had prophesied for me, and I was glad that it was now completed – not my pain, but Simeon's prophecy. No longer would I fear for my son's safety; I could now face the future with renewed energy. We had a mission to complete, given by my son:

'Go and make disciples of the entire world.'
What a task! I was eager to begin.
We will accomplish this.
All the world will know of Jesus, my son...

ACKNOWLEDGEMENTS

I would like to acknowledge the following people:

Rosemary Hooper and Lois Wollett – two dear ladies, both teachers, who proofread and corrected the first half of *Simeon's Prophecy* many years ago; Joanna Nicol and Morris Barling, who proofread the whole of my book; my husband, for his help and patience, in times of extreme tension; Andrew Killick, John Massam and all those at Castle Publishing, for their belief in my story and their generous help in getting it published.

Source material for this story was drawn from two books in particular: *The NIV Study Bible* (Zondervan) and *Jesus and His Times* (Reader's Digest Books).

QUOTED SCRIPTURES

This child is destined... Luke 2:34-35
The Holy Spirit will come... Luke 1:34-35
Joseph, son of David, do not... Matthew 1:20-21
Sovereign Lord, as You have promised... Luke 2:29-35
Why were you searching for me?... Luke 2:49
Go into the city... Matthew 26:18
I tell you the truth... John 16:20
My soul is overwhelmed with sorrow... Matthew 26:38
Simon, are you asleep... Mark 14:37-38
Are you still sleeping... Mark 14:41-42
Do you think I cannot... Matthew 26:53-54
Don't you fear God, since you are... Luke 23:40-41
It is finished... John 19:30
Do not hold to me... John 20:17